Praise for *The Butterfly Girl*

'*The Butterfly Girl* is a beautiful and very moving novel about lost souls. This heart-stopping thriller left me breathless'

Shari Lapena, author of *The Couple Next Door*

'Equal parts chilling, tragic and hopeful, Rene Denfeld's new novel combines her haunting, lyrical prose with a page-turning and harrowing mystery, putting *The Butterfly Girl* into a league of its own. Fans of *The Child Finder* will devour this'

Mary Kubica, author of *The Good Girl*

'There is a beautifully plangent, poetic quality to her depiction of a world that she knows all too well'   *Sunday Express*

'Vivid'   *The Sunday Times*

Praise for *The Child Finder*

'Poetic . . . Redemptive . . . Unflinching'

Barry Forshaw, *Financial Times*

'The sense of physical and psychological isolation is palpable in this moving exploration of loss, hope and human resilience'

Laura Wilson, *Guardian*

'Denfeld's haunting, disquieting and tension-filled tale is brilliantly told'   *Irish Independent*

'A truly mesm⸺⸺   *Heat*

RENE DENFELD is an internationally bestselling author, journalist, licensed investigator, and therapeutic foster mother. She is the author of the novels *The Child Finder* and *The Enchanted*. She has also written for the *New York Times Magazine*, *The Oregonian*, and the *Philadelphia Inquirer*. She lives in Portland, Oregon.

www.renedenfeld.com

Also by **RENE DENFELD**

The Enchanted
The Child Finder

THE
BUTTERFLY
GIRL

RENE DENFELD

WEIDENFELD & NICOLSON

First published in Great Britain in 2019 by Weidenfeld & Nicolson
This paperback edition published in 2020 by Weidenfeld & Nicolson
an imprint of The Orion Publishing Group Ltd
Carmelite House, 50 Victoria Embankment
London EC4Y 0DZ

An Hachette UK Company

First published in the US by Harper,
an imprint of HaperCollins Publishers

1 3 5 7 9 10 8 6 4 2

A CIP catalogue record for this book is
available from the British Library.

ISBN (Mass Market Paperback) 978 1 4746 0762 9
ISBN (eBook) 978 1 4746 0763 6
ISBN (Audio download) 978 1 4091 7538 4

Book design by Leah Carlson-Stanisic
Internal artwork by Mrs Opossum/Shutterstock, Inc.

Printed in Great Britain by Clays Ltd, Elcograf, S.p.A.

www.orionbooks.co.uk
www.weidenfeldandnicolson.co.uk

For Luppi, Tony, Markel, and Tamira.

Loving you gives me flight.

ONE

—

CATERPILLAR

Celia knew a bad place when she saw it.

The abandoned-looking house was in the industrial area next to skid row, where loading docks glistened with moisture and train tracks crossed the broken streets. The windows were covered with boards. What looked like blankets peeked out from under the slats. The front door was heavy and covered with locks.

Celia had been hunting for returnable bottles when she noticed the place. The few houses left in this area were usually empty. Not this one.

She balled her hands in the pockets of her jean jacket and studied the house. Her hair, dirty and musty, but still with a copper sheen, was cut short into wayward curls. She may have only been twelve, but she knew more than most. Or so she told herself. But deep inside her was the fear that she didn't know enough.

A shadow seemed to move behind the boarded-up basement window. Celia froze, then made herself breathe. Someone was looking at her through a tiny pane of glass. She could feel the heat of their gaze. For a second, it seemed that their eyes locked.

Celia disappeared inside herself. She was used to doing that. She could make herself vanish even as she stood there, just another street urchin with no future in sight.

Celia, who believed in nothing but herself and the butterflies, knew that the worst fears of the streets were always real. You can find this out the hard way, or you can be watchful. She backed away, and then ran back to skid row. But she could still feel those eyes in the window, burning into her with something that could have been anger—or might have been hope.

Naomi awoke, and for one brief moment, she thought she was back there. In the place. She heard her sister's voice, calling through the years: *Come back and find me. I'm twenty-five now. The water drips we once felt are gone, and the chariot has flown away.*

Naomi opened her eyes to find herself in her friend Diane's sunny guest room, curled with her husband, Jerome, in a bed once reserved for her alone during her rare visits. She breathed out in relief that the dream was over but still felt the anxious echo of the call.

I'm getting closer, she thought. This was why she was here in the city with Jerome. After almost a year of searching for her long-lost sister, their investigation had brought them here.

Her nose twitched. She could smell fried ham and coffee. The room was filled with sunshine, and Jerome was next to her, the cap of his shoulder rising against the sheet. In a moment she would get up and make her way down the narrow stairs to eat breakfast with her friend.

Diane served the ham with redeye gravy and scrambled eggs flecked with chives. Naomi poured cream in her coffee. She knew Jerome was probably awake upstairs but giving her these few minutes alone with Diane—she appreciated that.

Diane drank her own coffee black, wincing at the taste. She looked at Naomi's cream like it might spite her. "To be young," she said.

"You never worried before," Naomi said cheerfully, adding sugar to her cup.

Diane had aged in the last year. Silver laced her abundant red hair, and lines crossed her face. Her usual warm demeanor had quieted, and Naomi could see the loneliness in the slack skin under her jaw. And in her eyes.

"Staying long?" Diane said hopefully.

"Probably not," Naomi responded, cutting into her ham and tucking a piece into her mouth. "Thanks for letting Jerome come along."

"Of course. He's your husband." Diane said this mildly, but Naomi caught a whiff of disapproval. Disappointment with Naomi? The last time she had seen Diane was a year ago, at their wedding, right here in Diane's living room. Both Naomi and Jerome were thirty. It was their first serious—and for Naomi only—relationship.

She let it go, there among the matching breakfast plates with flowers on the rims, the linen-colored cups, the cream pitcher. Outside the birds were calling, and Naomi heard a crow silence them. She had been raised in the country and could identify a dozen birds by their sound. Yet she could not find her sister.

Diane's hand reached for hers. "You think she might be here," she said, softly.

"We heard about some missing girls," Naomi said, cautiously.

"One might be your sister?"

Diane knew that Naomi had escaped captivity as a child. For most of Naomi's life her only early childhood memory had been running through a strawberry field at night after escaping from a rotten trapdoor in the woods, deep in the Oregon farm valley. A group of migrants had found her and driven her to Opal, a small town an entire day away. Naomi had grown up there, with a loving foster mother named Mrs. Cottle. She was nine when she was found, but no matter how hard she tried, she could remember nothing more of her past. Terror had wiped her memory clean. Naomi had grown up to become an investigator, dedicated to finding missing children. She thought she wanted to find children like herself—but the real truth was that she wanted to find the little sister she had left behind.

Naomi shook her head. "I don't think so. They're too young. But I wanted to check it out. They were dumped in the river here. Those who have been found, at least."

Diane frowned, letting go of her hand. "I hadn't heard about that."

Naomi blinked at her plate. "The Green River Killer murdered at least seventy-five women. Dozens before anyone even noticed."

Diane looked sympathetically at Naomi. She knew how hard it must be to stay inside the center of the storm. "Were these prostitutes, too?" Diane asked.

"Street kids. Does it matter?"

"You know me," her friend said tartly. "Of course it doesn't."

Behind them, she could hear Jerome's soft descent from their guest bedroom upstairs. The man who had once been her foster brother, now her lover, friend, and more.

Diane reached for her coffee, sat back. She didn't know Jerome well.

Naomi looked up, smiled briefly. "Jerome. You explain."

The narrow form of her husband took a chair. He smiled at Diane, dark eyes on her, a hank of black hair falling. The shoulder cap of his missing arm—taken in the war—twitched. "We were visiting the task force in Salem when we heard street girls are going missing here. They're all Jane Does—even their street friends don't know their real names. Some have been murdered; their bodies have turned up in the river. Naomi wants to talk to her detective friend, visit the medical examiner, put up some flyers about her sister—rule out that she might have been one of the girls." He paused. "And maybe use her expertise to do something for these girls."

"I hope this all works out," Diane said quietly, blowing on the hot, bitter coffee.

Jerome reached with his one arm, found the cream pitcher with his long slender fingers, and, without asking, poured a rich stream into her cup. His eyes told Diane he understood what it was like to love Naomi. Diane found solace in his glance.

"Hope is enough," he said.

A heavyset man with a mashed face was watching Celia. He wore a blue jacket zipped up to his reddened neck, the kind of jacket worn by guys who work in automotive shops, only this one didn't have an I AM PETE name tag stitched on the front pocket.

He could be anyone. That was the truth of the streets: If there was danger, anyone could hold it. No one could be trusted, not in the end.

Celia believed this.

The beefy man, his eyes like tiny periscopes on her, could be *him*. The man prowling the downtown streets, making her friends disappear. Some turned up as corpses, floating in the river. Others just vanished. Not that such things didn't happen anyhow, but lately—in this heady spring of rain showers and streets that ran blood dark with freshets—it was happening more and more. Like all the time.

She stole another glance at him. His mashed face, pinched through the nose and eyes, was still watching her. Under his damp silvery hair, two funny-shaped ears protruded like little cabbages. His mouth was torn with scars.

Celia was down on skid row as dusk fell, the last of the business-people rushing, briefcases against their hips, like horses spurring themselves home. Oil puddles, sheened with water, made rainbows under the streetlights, and the night sky rushed away, reminding her the universe was vast. The gay bars were lighting up, the first of the cross-dressers coming out after dark when the night lights were kinder to their coarse faces, the stubble that the razors never quite got. Some had fake eyelashes so long they poked you when they came in for a hug. Which they liked to do, plenty.

She told herself she had nothing to fear. She had her friends for protection: Stoner and Rich, the two boys she hung around, street kids like her. Numbers in safety, Rich once joked. The boys were on the corner now, panhandling, their cold palms damp and empty. "Spare some cash?" they asked the suits whirling by. "I'm hungry, mister." Celia watched as the flood of commuters rushed down the street. Soon all that would be left would be the street people because the night was made for them.

She looked back over at the scar-faced man, but he was leaving. She saw his back and wet shoulders as he walked down the street. The brick wall where he had stood was empty. There was a dry shadow where he had been, like the outline of a shape from an atomic war.

Rich waved to her, a bill held triumphantly in his fist. "Some fool gave me a twenty," he bragged as she came closer. "Let's get some food."

Sometimes Celia thought she was a bird, flying over these

streets. Sometimes she felt more like a slip of air that could disappear, like the tendrils of mist rising from the gutters. But mostly, in her secret heart, she was a butterfly, with magic wings beating hard for escape.

* * *

That night Celia called her mom.

The other street kids didn't know she had a mom. None of them talked about that stuff anyways—it was too raw. Some of the kids said they were orphans, but Celia thought probably they were not. Orphans of the heart, maybe.

Celia borrowed a cell phone from another girl and tapped in the newest numbers written on the damp scrap of paper from her jacket pocket, fully expecting this number, too, would be out of service.

But the number was still alive. Maybe, too, the voice on the other end.

"Who is this?" her mom asked softly.

"It's me. Celia," she said, turning away from her friends. She remembered the first time she had heard the term *opioid addiction* and realized they were talking about her mom.

"My baby." In the background Celia could hear the television blaring. She strained to hear any sound of her sister, Alyssa. Now six, the same age Celia had been when her sister was born. The voice lowered. "I miss you."

"How is Alyssa?" Celia asked.

She could hear the airy high in her mother's voice. "She's fine."

When Celia talked to her mom her very pores cried with

sadness, and in just moments she became heady with despair, dizzy enough she had to reach for something to hold on to, which turned out to be the brick wall where she so often stood.

"You coming home?"

"You know I can't, Mom."

There was silence. She could hear her mother's slow breathing. Celia wished she understood this world, the things it did to you.

The other girl wanted her phone back—she poked Celia in her back with a broken nail. "I got to go, Mom. I was just saying hi."

Her mother yawned. "Celia. Is that you?"

Celia ended the call. A life can now be extinguished with the swipe of a finger. Then she went and sat on the curb, the car lights scoping the dark. The men in these cars, like her stepdad, were part of her. Her very cells had tasted them. Her blood coursed with them. But this was her life now, and she had to make something out of it.

*   *   *

Oh, the butterflies. They soften the edges of this hard world. Caught up so high in the sky, they fall to earth like meteorites, their iridescent wings trailing red thunder and liquid gold and the kind of purple only nature can provide.

Celia felt her back scrunch against her denim jacket, then relax. Sometimes she thought she had wings, bare nubs under the skin, and if others said these were her shoulder blades, she would say, Naw, that is where my wings are hiding. She could imagine the other kids along the row having wings, too, folded tight against their backs, wet and pulsating, opening now to feathered wonder. Bright green that flashed, the kind of silver that became light, white that became gold.

There could be legions of us, she thought, flying into the night sky. If all the street kids suddenly took flight, why, the night sky would glow with gold currents. Or maybe, she thought, it would just be her.

With a deep exhale, she flew.

Naomi understood that in investigations, the ground matters.

She had worked dozens of missing child cases, and each search began on the ground. It might be soft and dappled, with fir needles, as in one case of a Boy Scout who stepped off the trail. Or frosted and covered with snow, as in the case of a child gone missing in the Pacific Northwest woods. Or it might be rutted with concrete, a spill of black asphalt steaming on a city street.

The ground mattered because it led her someplace, always. She would find her sister on this earth because of the steps Naomi took on the ground. The thought filled her with impatience to begin.

Naomi knew to go to the darkest streets first. She went looking for the street people.

The place was called Sisters of Mercy, and it existed on a street known for winos and junkies. As night fell, Naomi passed crowds of street nomads, dusty in black leather, and skid row alcoholics with faces like bruised cherries. She saw a skinny old woman with tufts of hair on her balding dome digging through the loam of a gutter, cackling. There was a troubling number of families—mother, father, one or two kids, all with the tired, tense faces of poverty but not much else to say they were homeless but this: the long line.

It snaked around the corner, with the orderly discipline of the hungry. Having worked many missing cases involving the poor—they were usually the ones who needed her the most—Naomi had found they were the most orderly of all. Desperation was a profound governing force.

Cutting past the line, Naomi walked in the front door with scarcely a murmur behind her. That, too, was being poor. They were afraid of not being served, of going hungry. The empty café was filled with tables and rickety chairs, like any other restaurant. Only this one had a nun behind the counter, and her tired, warm eyes caught Naomi's.

"It's not time yet. Back of the line."

In the open kitchen, volunteers were busy cooking: giant vats of what smelled like beans and vast industrial sheets of cornbread coming out of the oven. At a table nearby stood self-serve jugs of water with paper cups. On the wall was a blackboard menu: *Rice, beans, and cornbread, pay what you can. Or work for your meal.*

"I bet you get a lot of dishwashers," Naomi said, stepping close to the counter. She pulled her investigator's license out, expecting the suspicion. "I'm not a cop," she said. "I'm looking for someone. My sister, actually."

The tired eyes met hers. There was a permanent wimple crease in the woman's forehead. "We don't talk about our customers."

"That's nice, that you say 'customers.'" Naomi smiled. "Usually I hear 'client,' like they are here on sufferance, or a boulder around our necks."

This nun apparently was not ready to be charmed. Naomi could feel the body across the counter, under the cloth: the exhaustion, the heavy-boned fight against injustice. "Look. I don't want to make trouble," Naomi said. "Do you have a community bulletin board where I could leave a message?"

There was a terse nod. Then the nun looked over Naomi's shoulder, and now she was genuinely smiling, because it was time. One by one the families and winos and street people filed in, and the nun's voice met each of them with a personal greeting, a name, or a question that sounded like love.

The bulletin board was in the annex of the soup kitchen, where Naomi also found a row of mailboxes so the homeless could get mail, as well as a message board plastered with notes. *Tony, brother, please call me*, read one. *Looking for my birth mom*, with details. Notices for AA meetings. Help for veterans. PTSD support groups.

And the posters for the missing street girls. Naomi read these with a chill in her heart. Most of the missing girls didn't even have real names—they went by street names like Mercedes and Diamond. Rich objects, dream worlds a life away. With relief, Naomi saw a name she trusted on the older posters: *Please call Det. Winfield, state police*. But underneath them were the crime stopper flyers for those found murdered, and these listed the number for the local FBI. Naomi frowned.

Naomi took a flyer from her messenger bag, the text circled in bright yellow so it would get attention. She pinned it in the center of the board.

I am looking for my sister. She is about twenty-five, the flyer said. Naomi had added the few details she could remember: the Oregon farm valley where they had been held captive, the bunker underground where a man had kept them, the year of her escape. She didn't know her own sister's name, so she couldn't add that. And then: *If you know her, tell her I am sorry and I miss her.*

Naomi stepped back.

An old man, querulous with alcohol or other shakes, had come up behind her, as silent as a whisper. Naomi could smell his gummy breath. He blinked, reading her flyer. "There's a lot of girls in this world," he said, grinning at her with horsey teeth.

"I know," Naomi said, huskily.

"What does she look like?" the old man asked, friendly.

"I don't know," Naomi had to admit.

"You ain't got a picture?"

"No."

"What kind of sister are you, to not even have a picture?"

Outside now the line was gone, the sidewalk empty. Behind her, through the dusty window, the tables were all full, the customers eating piles of the delicious-looking beans and the cornbread, cut in slabs and drizzled with honey at the table. A little girl with lank blond hair looked up at her. The mother touched her head, and the child's eyes returned to her plate.

Naomi felt tinny with despair. Night had fallen and she wanted to fall with it. She moved down the street, approaching every makeshift shelter and human sleeping in a doorway. "I'm looking for my sister," she began, each time, but at the end of the block she stopped, suddenly flooded with hopelessness.

This wasn't like her other cases. The fact those other missing children were not her family had allowed her to face the possibility they were never going to be found. Naomi understood now the panic of the parents, how they told her they couldn't breathe as long as their child was missing. Even in her sleep she was searching. If there was any chance her sister was connected to the missing street girls, she would find out. She knew from experience that those on the streets watched out for each other. They might help her.

She passed RVs crowned with tarps, a drunk retching on the curb. Tent camps that appeared overnight in parking lots, the wet sounds of sex in an alley. The lights of bars were ahead of her, the smell of exhaust, the sound of car doors opening and shutting. The red-light district. Naomi could see shapes of what looked like children, begging in the half dark. Begging and maybe something worse.

She moved towards them.

Celia was standing on the corner, the car lights white eyes in the dark. She hated the men in the cars, hated them and their reaching hands, their spongy needs, even as sometimes she, too, got in.

It was better than dying.

That was when she saw the woman coming down the street. The woman was medium-sized, not skinny and not fat. She looked strong. She had long silky brown hair that fell over her shoulders, and she pushed it back, impatient. Celia caught the wink of a ring on her hand. Her skin glowed in the night.

The woman clearly did not belong here, not in these days of sea creatures washed up onshore. What happened in the night was meant to stay secret—like what had happened with her step-dad, Teddy. Celia had made the mistake of telling. She had found out that the people of the day don't want to know what happened in the night.

This woman was a day person. Celia could see it at a glance, and her lip curled.

"Check her out," Celia said to Rich. The big boy looked down at his little friend, eager to see what sparked such scorn. Usually Celia was soft. Not now.

"Probably one of those church types," Rich said.

Celia's eyes were hard and green. "She should go home, then," she said.

The two watched the woman make her way down the sidewalk, talking with the other street kids. The cross-dressers were gone, blown away to the bars like so many drifting feathers from their boas. As the night got later, the people got smaller and harder, until the night whittled them away to nothing. Then it was time to run.

The woman walked into the street to talk to a kid. He was in the middle of what you might call a transaction, hanging in an open car window. The kid turned towards her, shocked at the intrusion, and behind the wheel Celia could see the astonished O of the john's mouth.

"What the fuck is she doing?" Celia asked.

"Maybe she's trying to find her good friend Jesus. He needs his nails redone," Rich cracked, and then looked disappointed that the sick joke had gone right over Celia's head.

Celia felt hot jealousy. She hated the woman instantly. To be so beautifully bold in the night—to walk and ask questions with her shoulders thrown back like she had the *right*. To act like she mattered.

Behind them their friend Stoner emerged from a car, all arms and legs, uncoiling until you could see his skinny height. His long limbs reminded Celia of how butterflies had six jointed legs so they could escape predators. It wasn't working for Stoner. He wiped his mouth, and no one said anything about where he had been, what he had done. He would feel the stain enough on his own.

"Let's go," Rich said, shifting his backpack. They left as the woman turned, the moon lighting her face into something beautiful.

The street kids crossed the river on the creaking footbridge, smelling the muddy water that ran thick below them. The cars on the bridge above them thudded by. Celia thought about the way life was lived overhead: the tall buildings, the big sedans, the groomed drivers. On the other side of the river rose the freeways, and under them a network of nests. The biggest was called the Caves. The homeless had tunneled underneath the concrete overpass, creating a labyrinth of caves. The Caves were ruled by rape, and the street kids stayed far away. Other overpasses were also viciously fought over, sometimes to the point of death: a crumpled body would roll off the freeway incline, only to be picked up the next day with a shrug by the city trucks.

Celia and her friends had no power and got no mercy from the others. They took what was left, the table scraps. But sometimes they found treasures, including a forgotten freeway ramp behind a closed paint factory, the entrance hidden by bushes. They called this place Nowhere. It was code, a way to keep this sleeping place hidden: *Where are you guys crashing tonight? Nowhere.*

The kids darted across the emptying freeways, between the whistling cars, until they came to the paint factory, then slipped under the torn cyclone fence around its parking lot. From there they climbed a steep hill to the overpass above, blackberry bushes tearing their hands. Where the rising freeway ramp met the dirt was a hollow the size of a small room. The ceiling was just high enough for anyone inside to stand up straight.

As they parted the bushes, Celia and her friends smelled old sweat and dust and urine. In the darkness they crouched, pulling food from their backpacks, gulping and tearing in their eagerness to be fed. They forced the food down in soft chunks, afraid even of the sound of their own swallowing. When they were done, they collapsed, simply falling over. But sleep didn't come, not for a long time. The boys lay wide-eyed listening to the cars passing overheard, and as night paled to dawn, these sounds became the metronome of their insomnia and fears. Every rustle of the wind in the bushes outside their cave was a night prowler.

Stoner put his long hand over his eyes and wept in the dark.

Celia lay awake, too. The air around her was blacker than darkness. She thought of the woman they had seen. She felt the jealousy return. The woman was going to sleep someplace, and it was not a dirt hollow under a highway, with spiders biting in the night. It would be a place with a bed that was safe. Not like her—or her sister, Alyssa.

Celia thought of Alyssa. She saw her stepdad, and her eyes glossed with tears. She made herself breathe deep. Butterflies never sleep, she remembered. They rest with their eyes open. This helped her calm down. She focused until she could see them in her mind, flying towards her, surrounding her with gentle flutters. Their wings cupped her ears, soft velvet on her cheeks, their tendrils tracing her closing lids, murmuring reassurance. More of them flew under the overpass, flying in great soft clouds until she was completely covered. They landed on her jeans, her tired feet, her empty middle. They drank her tears. They turned her into a cap of radiant color, and it was only when she was fully covered did Celia finally feel safe.

You don't want me coming with you?" Jerome asked Naomi.

It was morning, and they were standing on Diane's porch. The charming Victorian was painted bright colors. Their guest bedroom overlooked the street—Diane had the master in the back, above the quiet gardens. Naomi had met Diane when they both were testifying in a case. They became fast friends, perhaps because Diane accepted the way Naomi moved in and out of her life as she traveled the country for her cases. She had even let her store her case files in the empty attic.

But now Naomi and Jerome were broke. The past year had burned through what little savings they had been able to put aside. Naomi had refused to take on any other cases until she found her sister, and the travel meant Jerome couldn't find work either.

"We need some money, honey," Naomi said with a smile.

"I'm trying," he joked, flexing the one arm. The missing arm spoke for itself: You try finding work with one arm.

Jerome, who had been both a soldier and a sheriff, knew he was an excellent officer and investigator in his own right. But that didn't mean he was going to get hired into a local law enforcement agency, and he didn't know if they would stay in the city anyhow. He'd much rather live out in the country. But that conversation was waiting until they found Naomi's sister. If they didn't find her . . . well, he didn't want to think about that.

The one option he could think of was to become a private investigator like his wife. He wasn't exactly sure what Naomi would think of that. The failures of the past year had left them uncertain with each other. For the first time since she had come into his life, Jerome was hesitant to speak his mind with Naomi.

Jerome wished that someone had taught him how a marriage worked. Without a mother or a father, all he had known growing up was their foster mother, Mrs. Cottle, who, bless her soul, had been widowed. He wanted to be a good husband to Naomi.

She came closer, in for a hug. Surprised, he put his one arm around her, remembered the first time they had made love. Her face under him. "It's going to be okay," he told her, wishing he felt better about himself.

* * *

In Jerome's earliest memories of Naomi, she was a new child in their home, first scared but then full of bravado that slowly stilled into courage. Running along the rock ridges outside Opal, finding the miracle stones left by the petrification of time: quartz and jasper, shiny agates they polished with their shirts, and the ever-present opal. Spit and it will shine.

Their other favorite thing to do was search for old Native American artifacts. Parts of his heritage, like pieces of his own bones picked from the ground. Sometimes they found arrowheads—or what they pretended were arrowheads but were probably just triangular pieces of rock. A few times they found what appeared to be ancient campsites in the woods, with unusually large clearings where the plank houses might have stood. In such places were piles of rocks that did bring treasures, which Jerome was sad he had not kept. Horn spoons and rotting skin bags that fell apart at a touch.

Sometimes in the woods the fir trees gathered in a certain way, and Jerome could see on Naomi's face that there were things she was remembering even if the rest of her had to forget. At these times he took her hand and led her away. He distracted her by telling her about what he had read of his people—information that he would discover was true only some of the time—like how when his ancestors died, their families would tie their belongings in trees.

He and Naomi would walk back to the farmhouse, looking on the underside of every tree, hoping to see a relic from his ancestors. It didn't matter that they never found anything. He was with her, and that was what counted.

* * *

"If it isn't the child finder!"

Detective Lucius Winfield rose from his desk, one large hand held out, the office lights glistening in his short natural hair. Naomi smiled right back. She always felt comfortable in his presence. She took the leather chair, moving restlessly. Naomi could feel the clock ticking.

"What's up?" the detective asked. Winfield had known Naomi for almost a decade—they went back to her earliest missing child cases, some of which had been his cases. Parents often hired Naomi when police cases stalled. Winfield didn't mind sharing, if it got the job done.

"Still trying to find my sister," Naomi told him. She explained all they had done the past year, based on the slim handle of her memory. She told the detective how she and Jerome had combed old farm censuses, visiting dozens of strawberry fields in the Oregon farm valley. They had gone to Arizona and California to inquire after the makers of underground bunkers, seeing if there was a list of buyers. They had interviewed dozens of men imprisoned for stealing children. Her DNA had been swabbed and entered into databases to see if there was a match with unidentified bodies. They had even looked into international child trafficking. Nothing. She couldn't even find out who *she* was. It was as if she had been born the day she escaped, rising from the earth.

But then one day she and Jerome had stopped at a gas station on a country road deep in the valley. A truck of migrant farm workers had pulled up. The women and children were in the back, dark and swaying from the sun. They had pulled out empty plastic jugs to fill with water from the hose. It was Jerome, polished in Spanish, who struck up the conversation. An old woman, crossing herself, said yes, she remembered such a place. It had been an evil place, near a town called Elk Crossing.

"From there it was a race," Naomi told the detective. She and Jerome had finally found the fields, and the bunker in the forests nearby. But the rotten trapdoor was broken, the underground rooms empty. Her sister was long gone. Their captor, Naomi figured, had taken her sister away after Naomi's escape.

"I'm sorry," Winfield said, his voice full of sympathy. "It must have been awful for you to go down there."

Naomi nodded, swallowing the pain. "So we went back to the task force offices, and that's when I heard you got some missing street girls here. Some have turned up murder victims."

Detective Winfield leaned back in his chair, put his hand on his desk. "I should have known that would bring you to town."

"Five girls, all stabbed and found in the river," Naomi said. "At least a dozen other street girls have gone missing according to their friends. You could have another Green River Killer on your hands."

"I know," Winfield said. "We're drowning out there." He waved his worn hand at the city outside his office walls. "You've seen what it's like. Homeless all over the place. And all the ways the vulnerable get preyed upon. Trafficking. Crime. Disease. Murder. I'm up to my neck in cases."

Naomi frowned. "What about social workers and community agencies?"

"They're drowning, too."

"That why you gave the case to the local FBI?"

"I didn't give—they took." His voice was sharp. She saw a flash of anger. "You want to help, be my guest." His voice softened. "Look, we all care. I know you do, and so do I. But I can only do so much. I got over fifty open cases right now. How many you got?"

Stung, Naomi said nothing. She had exactly zero cases if she didn't include her sister. It was easy for her to judge. She felt bad and said so. "I'm sorry."

"Forgiven. If you find anything, if you need my help, you just say so," Winfield said, looking at his watch. "Now, I gotta go. You should go pay the Feds a visit. I think you might be surprised."

"At what?"

"You'll see."

Celia woke to a dome covered with the hieroglyphics of their times. Graffiti saying, *Sweet sickness. Dope. Death was here. Suicide?*

Stoner was at the lip of the overpass, pissing into the bushes. The sun filtering in the thick foliage looked bright. Celia had no idea what time it was. She wore no watch—watches were things of the past—and she couldn't afford a phone.

Her pockets were as empty as her eyes this morning, staring blankly out at the shimmering leaves, tipped with white shadows. Behind her Rich was still asleep, his arm thrown over his face, belly sloping against the dirt.

"Come on." Stoner came and kicked Rich in the leg.

Rich opened his eyes. "I was dreaming," he said.

"Don't tell me."

"Pancakes. A big stack of them, with butter and syrup. And orange juice."

"Fuck you, Rich," Stoner said. Rich rose slowly, groaning from sleeping on the hard ground. Celia shook out her dirty jeans and stomped the dust off her sneakers. Her denim jacket was as filthy as the rest of her. Sometimes she liked being dirty. It felt like she was part of the pavement, part of the city. Or nestled inside a cocoon, waiting for a brilliant birth.

She went to the corner of the cavern and lowered her jeans, pissing in the dirt. "I'm glad I'm not a girl," Stoner said, watching her.

"You're not?" Celia looked up, shaking her rump before pulling on her jeans.

"Ha." He tightened his belt.

Rich took his backpack and turned it upside down, showering the ground with crumbs. "I could swear there were pancakes in here," he said, and strapped it on his back.

Celia and Stoner picked up their empty backpacks. Celia felt her belly clench with hunger. Her stomach didn't even bother making noise anymore. It had learned silence like the rest of her. "Anyone got money?" she asked.

The boys looked away. No one wanted to say what they thought, which was Celia was a bit of a mooch. She was always begging and borrowing off the other street kids, and hardly turning any tricks or panhandling herself. Rich thought she used her tiny size as a charm. Anyhow, everyone was getting tired of it. "Maybe we should be asking *you*, Celia."

Stoner was the first one through the bushes, sending a white ray of sunlight back, piercing their night-shadowed eyes. Rich followed, and finally Celia, nursing her shame.

It always felt longer and hotter to walk back downtown in the daytime.

The street kids had to wait an eternity at the busy freeway, finally darting through the bawling cars. They walked back over the footbridge, the river below now pregnant with reflected light, the swells thick and hung with green particles of life. The smell was cold and fertile, like nature was waiting to give birth.

Nearby, in the industrial area, Celia could see the ancient docks reaching into the river. The waterfront there was muddy, torn up by cars. Johns went down there to park. Creeps, too. Celia tried to avoid it now, after seeing that scary house.

Skid row was chastened by day, empty bottles like holiday streamers in the gutter. The shelter doors were locked. They walked down to Sisters of Mercy, where it was almost time for lunch.

Celia had a powerful prayer for lunch. She wanted it to be served.

They were sweaty and tired by the time they reached the end of the line. Celia felt the hot sun melt the top of her head. It was an unusually warm spring day. Dark clouds lay in a sticky line on the horizon, promising a storm later. The air tasted like a copper penny, and Celia relished this, rolling the electric taste in her mouth.

The line moved slowly. None of the kids said anything. They shuffled. Somewhere behind them, two drunks started arguing and a man threatened to cut them if they didn't shut the fuck up. They did.

Shuffle. Move. Celia could feel the rough sidewalk through the thin soles of her shoes. She could feel each toe pressing down, holding her to the earth. Her mouth felt dusty. Even her ears felt closed, the canals thick. She was inside herself, a contented place to be, buzzing. Butterflies, she knew, live in a world of silence. They do not have to talk.

Rich touched her arm. Celia opened her eyes. He smiled at her, eagerly. She closed her eyes, ignoring him. She wasn't ready to be friends again yet.

Finally it was their turn. Given a plate each, heaped with the beans and cornbread and rice. They took the last table and sat with something like relief. Within moments the food was gone, and Celia stared at her empty plate.

"Are we gonna stay and help clean up?" Stoner asked. His voice sounded tired, like he was talking from the bottom of a deep well.

"Count me out," Celia said, scraping her plate to see if a stray bean might materialize.

"We said we would," Rich said. But when the boys got up, they found there was a ready line of dishwashers working off their meal.

"Come back tonight, to help with dinner," the nun said to the boys.

Celia wandered back into the annex. Her eyes were drawn to the message board and the posters for the missing and murdered girls, some of whom she had known. There in the middle, surrounded by yellow marker, was a brand-new flyer. She stepped closer, lured to it. Another missing girl, this time years ago. Celia shuddered when she read they had been held in captivity. *I am looking for my sister. Tell her I am sorry and I miss her.*

At the bottom was a name and number. Naomi, investigator.

"'Tell her I am sorry and I miss her.'" Celia tried the words out, saying them out loud.

They sounded funny—not ha-ha funny, but sad funny, like that was the last thing she expected anyone ever to admit in public.

*   *   *

In Celia's own memory she was six and her mother was pregnant. A girl, her mother announced, after a rare visit to the county health office. Celia was old enough to remember a time when her mother was a different person, the kind who went to doctors and even took Celia to the dentist, though they couldn't afford it. Somewhere, in her misty recall, was the feeling of her mom reading to her, the warm softness of her arm.

But then came Teddy. One of Celia's earliest memories was getting up late at night to pee and finding her mother on the couch with her white arm extended. Teddy, crouched as if he were proposing marriage, was sticking a needle in her mother's arm. Her mother had looked up, her eyes thick with sleepiness and guilt. She had been too high to even really notice her daughter.

But Teddy did, later.

He became the proud owner of a swollen drum of a belly he patted, lasciviously. And then it seemed like the day turned over and her baby sister was born. The infant lay in the hospital, wrapped in blankets. She had a dimple between her legs just like Celia, a confusing place of lies and secrets. From next to the hospital bed her stepdad had watched her, a warning on his mouth.

But Celia didn't want to tell, not then. What she wanted was to hold her baby sister, love her, protect her as she had not been protected. She had looked into her sister's sleeping face and promised, in her heart, that she would be her mother.

On the day they left the hospital, no one looked twice at the deflated mother, her eyes closed, sweat of withdrawals on her brow, the tall, lanky man next to her, his face grizzled with a red beard, or the little girl walking alongside, holding no one's hands but her own. Celia often walked that way, hands entwined in front of her like a monk on a stroll, and adults commented, chuckling, how it made her seem old and wise. They didn't know Celia clenched her hands like that to keep her limbs from flying off in fear.

Walking next to her mother and baby sister, Celia felt then, as she often did later, that she moved in and out of buildings and schools, waiting rooms and stores, and no one ever saw her. She was invisible, someone to be erased.

But her sister would be seen. Her sister, she promised herself, would be loved.

That night, on the row, Celia turned a trick. It was just her mouth, she told herself. You can always spit it out.

Her friends watched her climb back out of the car. The look in Rich's eyes was something like sadness. Celia strode up to him, holding out the money. "What I owe you," she said, voice hoarse.

"You can keep it," he said, face turning scarlet in the night. Behind them, loud in the dark, they heard sirens. Sirens all night, sometimes, until it seemed the streets turned into a puddle of flashing lights, spilled blood and mercy.

Some nights seemed made for magic, and this was one. It caught Celia unaware, like the hard breeze off the river, like the clouds rushing overhead. One moment she was standing on the sidewalk, rocking in her thin shoes, eyes half closed to the world, and the next a warm feeling swept through her body until her eyes blazed open.

Like she wasn't really a twelve-year-old street kid, ears closed against the crack of thunder. Like her mouth wasn't open to the pure cleansing rain.

The next morning, crossing the bridge, they watched the men on the patrol boat pull a body out of the river. It was a naked girl, as pale as a fish. The street kids stood at the railing and watched. A group of day people gathered on the esplanade nearby, and they, too, watched as if death were interesting to them, and not a little bit scary. One of them was the woman with the glossy hair. She had her arms folded as if she was enraged.

As the men on the boat hooked the body, Rich asked, "Do we know her?"

Stoner shrugged. "I think she was called Destiny."

The officers were touching the girl's body with more tenderness than she probably ever had felt.

Stoner was watching Celia with his sleepy eyes.

"We'll keep you safe, Celia," Rich promised, but Celia didn't say anything because she didn't think that was possible. It was one of those nice thoughts that had no power. The three of them walked slowly with their heads down away from the river as the boat churned water.

The FBI satellite offices downtown looked designed by someone with a degree in '70s kitsch: glossy mirrors, silver everywhere, burnt orange rugs. The modern desks and the high-tech computers reeked of money, and the receptionist looked like she was trying to fit in. Her silver eyes matched her hair.

"I'm here for Special Agent Richardson," Naomi said, sliding her license across the desk.

"Winfield said you would come," the agent said moments later, coming out into the waiting room, where Naomi was contemplating a recipe for stewed chicken in a cooking magazine. She wondered if there would ever be a day when she owned a kitchen and Jerome would come home to find she had stewed a chicken. Something made her doubt this.

Sean Richardson had glossy black hair that went with his title. He wore the classic Fed suit: pinstripe, with a neat little tie that suggested he was one tight asshole. Naomi disliked him instantly but had expected that: she and the Feds never got along. Unlike detectives like Winfield, they resented her for cracking cases they had spent years on.

He signaled at the chair. Naomi stayed standing. She looked out his window, at the river. "You were the one that solved the Nick Floyd case," Richardson said. He was annoyed at also having to stand, since he didn't want to sit if she wasn't about to.

Naomi glanced over. "I was glad to help," she said, gently.

"I read what you said about our office."

Naomi smiled, to herself. She didn't feel bad. Men like this were nothing. All she trusted in life was love, and none of it was here.

"I told the press that you are a bunch of bumblers who would make a beat cop look like a genius, and the only reason you get away with such ineptitude is the public has a bizarre and inexplicable belief in the FBI. I'm pretty sure they quoted most of that."

"All except the 'bizarre' part. No one likes to question the public."

Naomi turned. She saw the ghost of a smile on the man's face. Well. Maybe this was a new breed of special agent.

He came to the window. Both of them studied the river. "That's six now," he said, quietly.

He turned towards her. She saw his eyes were brown, and his eyebrows unruly. He had freckles on his cheeks. Another human. "I've got a good man on it, undercover," he said. "He's trying to break it from inside."

Naomi thought of the Floyd case. Nick Floyd was a generic-looking man who had led a generic-looking life, only he had kidnapped and murdered over twenty children. The previous FBI agent had fumbled the case badly, first releasing confidential information, then targeting a false subject for no other reason than that he was black and mumbled when he talked. By the time that poor man had finally been let out of jail, the trail had gone cold, and since the media had moved on, the FBI had tried to ignore the whole mess.

Naomi had been hired by the parents of one of the boys. It turned out the evidence had been under the agents' noses the entire time: a wet, almost indecipherable receipt from a feed store stuck in the bottom of the boy's backpack. The family owned no livestock. The receipt had led to a common point of intersection for all the children: the Floyd Family Feed Store, where kids were welcome to pet the baby chickens.

Naomi knew it wasn't callousness or indifference. The Feds just didn't have the right experience. They wanted to think men like Nick Floyd were smarter, more brilliant and cunning and unique than themselves. They didn't want to accept that the reason so many crimes against women and children went unsolved was not because a handful of brilliant sociopaths were outwitting the police at every turn. It was because people let such crimes happen.

It puzzled Naomi because she knew from experience that most people were good, or wanted to be good. They just couldn't see that fellow people were capable of being monsters, their own family and friends included. So they had to pretend such men were different, and in pretending they took away their own greatest power to stop them.

For Naomi, the men—and occasional woman—who took children were not her concern. The only thing that mattered was how they got away with it. They were doors to walk through to find the children. She refused to romanticize them by pretending they were extraordinary. This, she told herself, would include her own captor. If she found him—and finding her sister would probably mean finding him—she would look at him and know there was nothing special about him at all. She hoped.

"I still don't think you guys are right for it," she said. "Winfield knows more. Hell, I know more. Go back to busting PTA moms stealing the bingo money and claim it was first-degree embezzlement."

Sean Richardson surprised her by laughing. His brown eyes were on her, and he seemed delighted. Naomi suddenly felt mysteriously close to him. Maybe love was in these offices, too.

"Do you have a daughter?" she asked.

"No." He swung his hand towards the river, the city. "The world is my child. Funny, I know. But I feel that way. That's how I came to this work."

"I like you," Naomi said.

"Then you are going to leave well enough alone?"

"No."

* * *

For years Naomi had no memory of her captivity except for running through that strawberry field at night, her naked heels striking the black dirt. Running in terror to escape, only to turn back, horror filling her, not knowing why. Until one morning she had woken from sleep screaming a single word.

Sister.

After realizing she had left her sister behind, Naomi had expected that more memories would come—an avalanche of them, burying her in fear and regret. But that hadn't happened. What Naomi had willed herself to forget as a child had stayed forgotten. Maybe that part of her mind had erased the experiences, tossing them away like spoiled food. Or maybe the memories were waiting for when she was strong enough to access them.

Only one detail had come back. She was with her sister, deep underground, while the ceiling dripped. It was dark in the bunker, and a lamp cast yellow shadows. Her little sister was looking up, trust in her face, hazel eyes like her own.

Naomi was singing to her sister, softly. The lamplight flicked over them.

"Swing slow, sweet chariot," she had whisper-sung, "coming for to carry me home."

The song had a meaning that now filled Naomi with remorse. *If you get there before I do, tell all my friends I'm coming, too.*

It was a sin, Naomi knew, to forget. People stop existing once you forget them. Naomi had committed an unpardonable sin, and it didn't matter how many times others made excuses for her, like saying she had been a child or she had lived in terror. She had forgotten the one who mattered the most, and there would be no life, no future, until she found her. When she found her sister, she would beg forgiveness.

Naomi spent the rest of the day exploring downtown, hanging flyers in businesses and talking to people. Not just in the growing skid row district, where the street kids would prostitute themselves later. She walked all of it. The shopping malls, the delis and cafés tucked in the alcoves of buildings. She saw where the drug dealers hung out, and the addicts, and the women leaving department stores, wrangling large shopping bags and chattering like magpies.

Naomi thought about what it would be like to be one of the homeless kids she had seen. She wondered what it was like to live on the streets, where every doorway was a different hiding place, every tall man a knife.

On a deserted street back on the edge of skid row, she went into a corner market and got a drink. Outside she tried calling Jerome. His phone didn't pick up. She hoped it meant he was finding work. Maybe it was unfair to ask him to work, but the thought of not looking for her sister made Naomi feel sick at heart.

Dusk was falling, and a cold fog was rolling up the emptying streets. Walking along the street, Naomi found the downtown public library. The stone facade was lovely, damp with the mist.

Public libraries were often places where street people hung out.

She would talk to the librarians and post some of her flyers.

Celia was in the library. It was her favorite place to be, besides her own imagination.

She perched, sneakers swinging, in one of the wood chairs. The hard chair didn't bother her. Nothing bothered her in the library. Her head floated up to the clouds, the ornate ceiling above, and when her hand touched the burnished rails of the marble staircase, she became part of the world.

The best part of the library was becoming one with the butterflies.

She carefully turned a page. She was reading her favorite book on butterflies, the one with the dull blue cover that gave no hint to the treasures inside. The edges were grayed to the point of silver. Like the dust of butterfly wings, Celia thought. The elderly librarian kept this book behind the counter just for Celia. It was a secret they shared—a good kind of secret. Once, when she was in third grade, a neighbor had invited Celia to her house for soup. The librarian reminded Celia of that neighbor. It helped her remember there were nice people in the world. She didn't blame them for what happened. They were too busy taking care of each other.

Celia could spend hours inside the book. She touched the color plates with her dirty fingers. The butterfly colors leapt off the page: a skyrocket of red, the brightest blue you ever saw, the gold of a perfect sunset. On pieces of scrap paper nearby she drew pictures of the butterflies, some fantastical, some real. When she was done, she tucked these inside the book, like treasures.

"Celia?" It was Rich, in a hoarse whisper. Rich hated the library. He said the library made him smell like piss. Of course that wasn't really true; it was just the warm, dry, close air that made it obvious. Celia didn't tell him this.

"You can go. I'll come later," she told Rich, who put down his comic book.

"It's almost dark—" he began.

"I'll catch up to you. You know where." Celia was lost in the butterflies.

Rich left. It was getting wet and cold outside, moisture dripping from the building eaves. The last of the day people were leaving their offices, hurrying through the darkening mist. Overhead a giant black clock ticked. Seven o'clock.

In the room above him, Celia was swinging her feet, smiling and reading. She pulled a piece of paper forward to draw another butterfly.

Outside the man with the mashed face and cauliflower ears was waiting. He saw Rich leave. The girl was alone, inside.

* * *

What is it you want?

When the butterflies talked to Celia, it was like the sweetest notes of music. She could hear them coming from afar. She could see them now, covering the misty library windows. They were above the fantastic chandeliers, flying all around, as thick as fabric flowers above the bowed heads of readers. She named them as they passed: painted lady, swallowtail, viceroy, brush-footed, gossamer. The original brimstone. Metalmarks, hairstreaks, nymphs, and skippers.

There was no creature at all like the butterfly—they were unique animals unlike any other. It wasn't just their wings, covered in thousands of tiny reflecting scales. It was the truth of their complex bodies, their all-seeing eyes, their feelers. They landed on the table and smiled at her, tapping with musical feet. She smiled, drawing a wing.

Sometimes the butterflies sang to *her*, Celia, and their songs were like bits of music, the sound of a piano maybe. A single finger on a key, the note hanging in the air, too pretty to fall. Celia's eyes filled with tears as the butterflies gave voice to her own wonder.

I want to be okay, she answered the butterflies. And the butterflies said yes, of course. They had promised this, from the time before she was born. They had made her mother promise this, too, before it was too late and the darkness overtook her.

One, two, three. Look!

The library lights flickered on and off above her, and the butterflies startled, rising in thick clouds. It was time to go. Celia slid her drawing into the book, gave it a kiss, and rose. Like the others with nowhere to go, she went down the stairs.

* * *

Having a baby sister had changed everything in Celia's world.

Before, she became a wooden tree left in the bed where Teddy came on nights when her mom passed out on the couch. He put his thing into the hollow of the tree trunk, then held its lifeless branches until he groaned. But then her sister was born. During those long days when her mother slept, or sweated and moaned, waiting for her fix, it was Celia who rocked the baby, changed her diapers, learned how to mix the formula, and later, standing on a stool at the stove, boiled the carrots she mashed, testing with her own tongue to see if they were cool enough for the baby to eat. It was Celia who learned to read so she could understand the words in the Dr. Spock book she had found on the living room bookshelf. It was Celia who called the ambulance one night because she misunderstood the thermometer and thought her baby sister was dying of fever. Her mother, she explained to the ambulance driver, had the flu. That was why she slept through the entire incident.

It was because of her sister that Celia discovered time. Before she knew it, her infant sister was kicking in the dirty high chair, sucking on a pork-chop bone. Then she was two, and three, playing with pots and pans on the floor while Celia stood on a stool at the stove, cooking dinner. Celia, too, grew in these years, but she never stopped being a tree.

It had happened when Alyssa was five and Celia was eleven. She watched her sister change from being a baby to having a shape around her mouth, to having legs that lengthened and arms that took on a honeyed hue in the sun. She had the same copper hair as

Celia, only lighter. She's a pretty girl, strangers started saying, and deep in Celia the alarm sounded.

Make it me, Celia prayed. I will be the tree.

One day Celia took Alyssa out in their backyard to look for butterflies. The backyard had not been mowed for years. Celia liked it this way. There were little garter snakes in the grass, and baby toads, and sometimes the most precious of all, butterflies. "Butterflies are magic," she told her sister as they hunted carefully in the tall grass, Celia whispering the names when they saw the ones she could identify.

A shadow fell over them. It was Teddy, come home from work. Teddy worked construction, and it was his money that bought the dope her mother now needed. Her mom was as captive to Teddy as Celia was captive to being a tree. He was standing behind them, a fresh beer in one hand, scratching his belly with the other. His blue eyes were on Alyssa. And in that moment, Celia saw how her stepdad was looking at her baby, the speculation in his glance. The planning. *No*, her heart cried, I will not let this happen.

The next day she went into the nurse's office at school and reported what was going on at home. She knew exactly what she was doing; she was telling on Teddy to save her sister. She was going to save all of them.

It was the greatest mistake of her life.

Naomi was climbing the steps to the library when a teenage boy came out. He had the unwashed look of a street kid, and his furtive glance, his eyes widening slightly, told her she was on the mark. She reached out, but the boy lowered his head and hurried off. The evening was getting cold, more rain clouds coming.

It was then she saw the man. He looked like a former boxer, his eyebrows broken with scars, his lips thick with keloids. He wore a blue repairman jacket, zipped up, old trousers, worn shoes. Silvery hair hung down to his chin. Not quite down-and-out, the look said. Dangerous. The man felt dangerous to her.

The man looked back at Naomi indifferently. His thick lips smiled, but it was a cold smile. He was standing under a small alcove sheltering him from the misty rain. Like he was waiting for someone.

Naomi went inside.

"We're closing," the librarian said as soon as she entered, not even looking up from her desk. She was absorbed in a worn paperback copy of *The Shell Seekers*, by Rosamunde Pilcher. Naomi smiled. It was one of her favorite comfort books, too.

"I have some flyers," Naomi said, coming closer. "And a few questions, if you don't mind." She showed her detective license. The librarian put down her book, sliding a homemade crochet bookmark in place, and then put on the sparkly glasses hanging on her neck, leaning over.

A girl was coming down the marble stairs, holding a thick book. She was small and slender, wearing a dirty jean jacket. She had a heart-shaped face under a mop of messy hair, and her green eyes seemed to view the world with trepidation. She was absolutely filthy. Naomi saw a stain of dirt on her cheek as she came closer.

A part of Naomi pinged. She remembered only too well thinking they wouldn't notice you hiding behind the dirt. But it never worked that way.

The girl glanced at Naomi, then quickly looked down. She slid the book back over the desk. Naomi caught a glimpse of the title, something about butterflies, and saw how the pages were stuffed with pieces of scrap paper. She thought of her own fascination with the wilderness after escaping captivity. The outdoors represented more than nature. It represented freedom.

The librarian smiled gently at the girl. "Thank you, Celia. See you tomorrow?" The girl nodded shyly. The librarian reached under the desk and, with a conspiratorial wink, passed the girl a small jar of nuts. Blushing with pleasure, the girl took it.

The girl cast a green-eyed glance in Naomi's direction that was hard to read, and then hurried for the big black doors. The librarian watched her leave. She sighed. "I wish I could take her home," she said. "I wish I could take them all home."

Naomi remembered the man on the steps. "Excuse me," she told the librarian, leaving the flyer on the desk to go after the girl.

Outside the mist was catching the streetlights, flickering with reflected colors. Shadows marched up and down the empty streets like the legs of monsters. The girl was at the bottom step, moving fast, with the energy of youth.

The scar-faced man had left the stoop. He was trailing her.

* * *

Celia, unable to contain the excitement of a world that brought butterflies and rain, almost danced in her movement. She raced towards a group of pigeons, waving her arms and sending them to flight: gray and magenta, tipped with a green so brilliant she couldn't help but smile. The pigeons made a sound like the best of mothers, cooing, and in Celia's mind they were cooing at her.

The man behind her melted into the shadows so easily that even Naomi, an expert tracker in her own right, was impressed. Impressed and more than a little scared. Not for herself but for the girl.

Naomi was aware of how empty the streets were here. A child could be grabbed, easily, and hustled into a dozen hiding places. The girl was about a block away, the man still trailing her. At any moment they might turn a corner and disappear.

Naomi began to run.

At the very last moment the man heard Naomi and spun around, light flashing on his scarred knuckles. The expression registering on his broad, pebbled face was one of consternation. His mouth opened, but then closed. Backing up quickly, he moved with surprising grace and ducked into an alley. He was gone.

Breathing heavily, Naomi stopped. The girl had whipped around, too, backing up a couple of steps while taking everything in. She quickly covered her fear with a protective sneer. The streets were silent.

"Your name is Celia, isn't it?" Naomi asked.

"How did you know?"

"The librarian. She said, 'Thank you, Celia.'"

"I remember you from the row," the girl said. "The church lady."

"What makes you think I'm a church lady?" Naomi asked, catching her breath. She smiled now, at ease.

"I saw you down there. You don't belong."

"Belong here, or there?"

"Anywhere."

Taken aback, Naomi thought: She's like a messenger. A messenger from my past, speaking my own sins, my fears. The girl was staring at Naomi with the kind of hate that comes from envy. Just for a moment Naomi saw it: she wants to be like me, but she's afraid she never will be. The night had come up behind the girl, darkening her ears, catching the copper of her hair. Soon it would be pitch black, and a girl like this—well, she could disappear.

"I was worried for you, with that scary man following you," Naomi said. "I'm an investigator. I specialize in finding missing children."

A blink. No response. Naomi was close enough to see the lines of dirt on her grimy neck. She wondered when this kid last had a bath.

"How old are you?" she asked. "What's—"

The street boy Naomi had seen earlier had reappeared down the street. The little girl turned and saw him, and her whole face collapsed in relief. She's afraid, Naomi thought. She doesn't know who to trust. I don't blame her.

I know what her life has been like.

I'm glad I came back for you," Rich said to Celia.

They were on the row, in the circus of lights. A bunch of frat boys were downtown, and the air was sharp with them. Celia preferred old men, for the times she had to. Old men were soft and called her "darling" and "little baby." They wanted to pretend she was their daughter. It was gross, but something Celia told herself she knew.

Young men—they were made of blades. They liked to hurt, and skid row turned into a bloodbath when they were downtown.

"Thank you." Celia came forward and leaned her face against his chest. Rich froze. In his wildest dreams Celia was doing exactly this. He lifted up his arms, slowly, to capture her, but she moved away. The moment was gone, stolen by the night. It was almost like it had never happened. Rich felt sick with despair. Nothing in this life was made for him.

"Hey, ya fat fag," a frat boy called out of a car, as if to prove the point. The other frat boys hung out of the windows, faces wet with drink. Rich imagined scythes cutting close to the car, taking them all off at the waist, their bodies falling with a clunk, lips and blinking eyes able to say no more.

"You're not gay, are you, Rich?" Celia asked, curious.

No, he shook his head, and his very soul ached with loneliness.

That night it was like a party on the streets. Rich and Stoner were there, of course, but so was everyone else and more. Bags filled with glue, to be huffed in the dark alley shadows. Someone carrying a gas can up a street clogged with cars. A junkie falling in a fit, drunks with wet groins, one of the frat boys vomiting against the wall while his friends, all in polo shirts, pitched bets and urged more.

Sometimes Celia hated life. She hated it even as it unfolded, even when it seemed so wondrous. The night sparkled and showed her more:

A man saying "Touch this" and "You get a dollar, my sweet," and looking down to see the bulge of his groin, hearing his manic giggle. Dancers swaying with arms around trannies and slim-hipped boys in the night. Wondering what was in her drink, the soda someone—was it a friend?—had passed her. Black cherry cream, her favorite.

Sometimes the streets felt like acid. You didn't need to drop it to know this. You could crawl in the gutter, taste the same dank butts as anyone else, marvel at the view. You could stand below strip club lights, seeing the whirl of a dozen lovely girls—and hear the catcalls of the men outside. Their voices were rich with want, heady with sweat and something she could not name but hoped was love. That's all she wanted.

She felt hands grabbing her, pushing her towards the entrance, saw the security man at the door, smirking. He was large and had a greasy smile like Teddy, and this set off alarm bells in her. Celia jerked back, trying to get away. The men outside, drunk on lust, swung her around, catching her in their tangled arms and rude laughing faces, ugly teeth yellow and crooked, until suddenly she felt a hand on her and—

Everything stopped.

"I got you." It was a small man in a tidy suit. In her befuddled state Celia saw only a slim dart of a being, with blue eyes flashing behind round glasses. He had bright silver hair, cut short at the sides, and looked far too elegant for the streets.

"Hey." It was Rich, and he was reaching for the sodden Celia, and the nice man handed her over, smiling tightly. Celia crouched at the gutter, vomiting.

"I think someone spiked her drink," the man told her friends. "She ought to be careful of what she drinks on the streets."

"What happened?" Celia asked what felt like hours later, wiping the wet from her chin, aching all over. The sun was coming up.

"Let's go sleep," Stoner said, circles of exhaustion around his eyes.

Which was how Celia woke up to the concrete dome of the overpass above her. She was lying on her back in the dirt, the smell of urine around her, and above, the thud of passing cars counted out the time. When she felt this sick, it was hard for the butterflies to come, and this alone was reason not to do drugs or drink. The butterflies might abandon her forever, just as they had her mother.

* * *

One butterfly.

She was in a courtroom, shaking. The victim advocate—a booming woman who kept saying everything would be all right—had told her just to take the stand. Tell the truth, they all said, but how can you tell the truth when the lie is right in front of you?

Teddy.

Two butterflies.

It took most of a year even to get there. Can you imagine? A year of her mother crying, listening to Teddy on the jail phone saying he had done nothing, she would know if he had, wouldn't she? And her mother finally saying yes. The addiction not going away but getting worse, fed by the money Teddy sent. Two candles her mother put on the mantel. "We are going to light these every night Teddy is in jail," her mother said, as the candles flickered, and the look she gave Celia was haunted, like she had made a choice she had since forgotten.

Three butterflies.

Celia losing herself in the maze of lies, questioning her own reality, watching her mother talk to social workers, telling them it couldn't possibly be true. Celia knew her mother couldn't tell anyone about the syringes under the couch, about how the drugs had taken over her own life. She might go to jail, too. Celia in the bathtub with a strainer in her hand, watching the water pour through the holes. Who was telling the truth?

All Celia had to do was look at her sister to know she was.

Alyssa, her beloved. Taken by child services because of the allegations of sexual abuse in the home. Why did they leave Celia then? Not enough foster homes, especially for older kids, she was told. Teddy was in jail, they said. Celia was safe. They didn't know her mother, how strong her addiction was, how open her veins were to Teddy's lies.

Four butterflies.

Alyssa finally coming home. Different. Smelling of laundry soap from another home. Having learned to wipe her mouth as she ate, all dainty like. Flossing her teeth every night, which Celia never did, and she felt guilty and angry she wasn't the one who had taught her. Talking about her foster family like they were the ones who really loved her, saying they had wanted to adopt her and she hadn't wanted to come home.

"Light a candle for your father, dears. The one *Celia* put in jail."

Five butterflies.

That final day in court. Led to the witness chair by the victim advocate, her hand imprisoning Celia's wrist. Celia sitting down, quaking, seeing Teddy there, in a suit next to his public defender. The lawyer had stood, smoothing out his jacket.

"Miss Celia . . ." The attorney had stepped forward, victory already in his eyes. "What does your family call you?"

She had felt the roof of her mouth with her tongue. Looked over the people in the pews, all looking back at her. The judge was a black vulture at her back. In the midst of all this was her mother. She sat with her head bowed. She wore a pretty new dress, long sleeves over the marks. Her eyes looked up, full of guilt that ran to the bones.

Six butterflies. As old as the sister you will lose.

"They call me Celia the liar," she had said, and was surprised at how clear it came out.

Naomi had put up flyers, visited her detective friend, paid her call to the Feds. Seen some street kids, asked around about shelters.

It was nothing, she told Diane in her mind, driving to her house in the puttering Datsun. By the time she got in the door the echoes of her mind were no longer soft and listening, but hard and frustrated.

"I'm not doing anything on this case!" she barked to Jerome and Diane, both in the kitchen, looking up from the homemade pizza they were taking out of the oven. Jerome's eyebrows rose, and Diane's merely arched. Her entire being said, Don't even.

"You mean your sister or the street girls?" Diane said, wiping her floury hands on a towel. Jerome glanced from where he was testing the pizza.

"Both." Naomi pulled out a chair hard.

"Mind your manners."

"I'm not five."

"You're acting like it." That was Jerome.

Naomi whipped on him. "Maybe you should get a job."

Dead silence followed that. The whole kitchen took on a polar chill. Naomi felt the tick of shame in her belly, the rising fear. She wanted to apologize, but Jerome turned and left to go upstairs. She had never seen the look he had on his face before. It wasn't even anger.

It was distance.

"Naomi. Honey." Diane was coming to her, moving her hands toward her head. Naomi leaned in, unwilling. "I'm sorry," she murmured, against Diane's hair, once so silky, now brittle. Naomi could feel something, deep in her friend, something that felt like sadness, but in her own distress she let it slip away.

"It can only take a minute to ruin a lifetime, my dear." Diane's voice was firm against her. Her arms held Naomi tight. "Just like your cases. It only takes a minute to ruin a life."

Naomi collapsed. The anger ran out of her. She fell into the chair, crying helplessly into her hands. "I keep trying," she kept saying.

Diane lowered herself carefully and held Naomi's knees. "Trying to do what, my dear?"

"To remember."

"And you think you need to?"

"I don't know."

"You think you failed because you haven't found the one you think matters the most. But Naomi. My dear. Your sister isn't the one who matters the most."

Naomi lowered her hands. Her face was wet with tears and hard with fear. "Who does, then?"

"He's upstairs right now. The future."

Naomi stood up so hard the chair knocked over. She left the house.

They didn't talk for two days. Them—once foster siblings, running in meadows, fashioning whistles out of split grass, teaching each other how to skip stones play leapfrog jump rope double dutch fly-fish do algebra drive a tractor look in my eyes now Naomi. Two children who once couldn't go ten minutes without a serious smile or giggle, who fell asleep telling each other stories—now silent.

At one time, not long after their marriage, when as adults they had realized the truth of their love, Naomi had woken up thinking she had swallowed Jerome's missing arm and was going to make it for him, like a paper wasp spits a nest, and when she told him this, he had merely smiled, and looked at the empty space his arm would take, and said, "I can see it already."

I wanted to be your future, she thought.

You are making me the past, he thought.

Diane's thoughts whirled in her room, trying to figure out a way to make things right between Naomi and Jerome. But she knew better. The silence in the house was two young people stuck in a sea of stubbornness. Like so many of their era, and maybe like people of all times, they had no role models.

Naomi's entire body was filled with self-loathing when she and Jerome were not talking. Naomi, too, remembered the hunts for artifacts that she now suspected were more about love than arrowheads or bundles in trees. In Jerome's own child face she had seen the hunger for a place to call home. He didn't know how deep her own longing ran, or the terror. For Naomi, home could be a prison.

But it had happened anyway. One day—whether looking into trees for treasures tied in the branches or picking up agates on the ridges—she had fallen in love with him, and it had taken her most of her life to admit it.

Not knowing what else to do, she made a list:

Jane Doe bodies, morgue
Psychiatric hospital? Maybe she was committed.
Stop in/visit every homeless shelter

And last but not least:

Who is that man? The one with the scars.

Riding the bus made Celia sleepy. She closed her eyes, putting her cheek against the soothing chill of the window glass. She folded her hands inside her thighs and dozed off. She was aware of the warm bus, the smell of other poor people around her, someone playing loud music through their ear pods.

She was on her way to visit her mother.

At stops she heard the accordion hiss, felt the bus lower. She was counting the stops as she dozed, feeling back in time as the distance between stops got longer and glimpses of yards furred with weeds and grass, gnarled apple trees, and gutters rusted with moss ran through her mind. In her dreams she was running beside the bus, feeling the wind in her lungs. Then she was tired and rode back inside her body. The butterflies, floating against the window, were tapping. Celia, they said. You are no liar. You never were. Remember that.

"Mom?" She stood on the dime-sized concrete porch, peeking in the broken screen door. Inside was a haze of stale cigarette smoke and the din of the television. "Mom?" This time louder, a little squeak in her voice.

"That you, Celia?"

Her mother's voice was hoarse with sleep and sickness. Celia could tell in that moment her mother was on the same afghan-covered sofa. It felt like Celia's heart broke and fell to the ground in pieces, so much she had to crouch to scoop them up and shove them back in her chest.

"Yeah. It's me." She saw her hand reach out, slowly. She heard the creak of the screen door, paused. "Teddy isn't here, is he?"

Silence. A quiet no.

An hour later, Celia stood at the sink, washing dishes. She had picked up the floor, swept cigarette butts, cleaned the foul mess of the litter box. One of the cats was nowhere to be seen, and her mother, slipping in and out of her nod, couldn't seem to remember when it went missing. Celia hoped it hadn't been hit by a car. Maybe a nice neighbor had taken it.

Her mother lay on the couch, a dried-out washcloth over her face. Celia took it, wringing it out with fresh cold water and putting it back. Her mother sighed. Celia picked up ashtrays and the dirty clamshell takeout containers with petrified fried rice.

"That you, Celia?" her mother asked again.

Celia stood and looked at her. She didn't know why she kept coming back. Nothing changed. She remembered a junkie on the street telling her that his brain felt like a fuse, burned out and dry. Maybe her mom had lost her memory, too.

"It's me, Mom, remember?"

"Oh." Her mother turned her head. "Can't you come home, Celia?"

"We've talked about that, Mom. You know I can't."

"Teddy would forgive you."

"I didn't lie." It took all of Celia to say it. Her mother's disbelief was like a stone in her throat. Her whole stomach felt filled with the sickness of it. Her mother's mouth moved, but no words came. After a moment, they did.

"That's not what the jury said," her mom whispered.

Celia went into the tiny, messy bathroom. Using her mother's scissors, she hacked at her hair until it was short again. She liked looking more like a boy—it was safer on the streets. She went back to cleaning the kitchen and left when she was done.

The pavement behind the school was broken with time, sprouting grass from the cracks like whiskers on an old man's chin. The metal bars of the jungle gym, glossed by decades of dirty hands, cast long shadows.

Celia was hungry. She should have tried to find something to eat at her mom's house. She thought of the always dirty, crowded fridge, the bags of old meat leaking brown juices. The last thing she was able to teach Alyssa was to make sure and ask the lunch lady if she could help for extra food.

She saw her sister coming out in a group of other girls. Celia was always too dirty, too ashamed, for friends. And once she had reported, everyone knew. *Fuck bag*, some of the boys called her, and tried to stick their fingers up her shorts. *You already did it, so what's the big deal?* Celia hadn't worn shorts since.

Her sister saw her. An uncertain smile. Celia, filthy in her street clothes, aware now that she smelled. Maybe she was her mother after all. Just dirty in another way.

"Hi, Alyssa," Celia said. The other little girls tittered nervously. Alyssa stared up at her sister, and her friends left to find their parents. Celia and Alyssa were alone on the blacktop.

"You look nice," Celia said.

Alyssa was wearing a decent shirt and cleanish pants. Celia could imagine her, closed into their bathroom, trying to stay clean. She had been brushing her hair, but had missed a big spot in the back, and there was a knot. Celia reached for it, but Alyssa jerked away.

Why not you? Celia wanted to cry out. She had done everything to save her sister, yet her sister hadn't needed to be saved. Was there something wrong with Celia? Had it all been for nothing?

Acquitted, the victim advocate had told Celia after the verdict. She had to explain what the word meant. "You mean he is coming home?" Celia had asked, terror grabbing her throat.

The very next day he did, and Celia couldn't go to school for a week for the beating that followed his return. Celia didn't wait for the next beating. Or rape. That was the only good thing she got out of the entire trial—she learned the right words for what Teddy had done. That night she had taken her backpack, some clothes that were soon stolen, and ridden the bus downtown. She had been lucky enough to meet Rich while she was wandering the streets, trying to look tough when really she was so scared.

All for nothing. Because now, as her sister stood before her, Celia didn't think Teddy had ever touched her. Not in that way, at least. Alyssa was looking up at Celia with something like suspicion. No doubt she was thinking what everyone else said: that Celia had made it up. The jury had said so.

But it was true, Celia wanted to say. I told to save you.

All the way back downtown—walk, buses, walk—Celia engaged in her favorite pastime, which was to daydream. "Dream by day," her teacher Mrs. Wilkerson once told her. "Dream by night. Your imagination can save you, Celia." Reality is whatever you chose to see: the face of a gnome in the grass, a construction team of elves on an anthill, the way tree leaves lace together to make messages only you can read.

And yes, the butterflies. They cascaded around her now, tickled her tired feet, lifted her shoes all the way back to the bus stop. They rode next to her through the bus window. As she got off downtown, one grabbed hold of a strand of her hair. Celia laughed. She could remember being a little girl in a sun-splashed meadow with her mother. She could feel her wings open.

What are you doing, Celia?

Flying, she told the imaginary person in her mind.

Arms out now, running through the downtown streets, seeing the shocked faces of the day people as she passed. Celia the butterfly, brilliant green, blue, red like a star. Celia the truth.

Rich looked up to see his friend running down the middle of skid row, her arms stretched out, a glorious look on her face. It was funny—he could almost see the shine of her wings. People stood back, watching her fly.

Celia. Just Celia.

The city morgue had, at one time, been set near a community center, and across from a bookstore selling used library books. Naomi had visited the facility on other missing child cases that brought her to the city. She had found it a friendly place, with attendants bustling in their greasy plastic aprons, a pot of coffee stewed to sharp bitterness on the counter, and a plate of cookies no one wanted to eat. The old place had been associated with all sorts of scandals, including an attendant caught taking dried blood home to fertilize his roses.

The new building had been built out in the suburbs, possibly to clean that stain. It sprawled, all pale stone, and yet the refrigerator chill was more obvious. There were no more strange cookies in the waiting area. There was only a fan circulating the muddy air.

The medical examiner was a quiet man named Mike Morton whose hobby was making model airplanes. One for every case that haunted him, he had once told Naomi—now he sat behind a desk so crowded with flying machines it might take off with him. Maybe that's what he wanted, Naomi thought.

"Child finder," Mike said, rising quickly to shake a hand.

Naomi smiled at her nickname and sat down. Mike Morton was a small man, made smaller by his work. His skin was the same gray color of the bodies he worked on.

"I'm looking for my sister," Naomi said, and explained.

"If you've entered your DNA into the system, I don't have anything new for you," Mike said. Naomi felt some relief, but not much. In her heart she was convinced her sister was alive.

"I had assumed you were here about the murdered street girls," Mike said.

Naomi hesitated. No one had hired her officially on the case, but no one was stopping her either. Now that she had met some of the street kids—Celia especially—she felt responsible. She told herself it wasn't hurting to work that case while searching for her sister.

"I thought you might have some ideas how to identify them," Mike said.

Naomi remembered her foster mother, Mrs. Cottle, and how hard she had fought to get Naomi a legal identity. Like so many children who ended up in foster care, Naomi didn't have a birth certificate. If she had run away or been kidnapped before Mrs. Cottle managed to get her a social security number, there would have been no way of tracking her, just like there was no way of tracking her sister.

"I'd check with child welfare," she told him. "Maybe those girls were in foster care before they became homeless. That could be why you're coming up empty."

His eyes widened. "What a good idea. Thank you. Would you be willing to look at them, tell me what you think?"

Naomi hated looking at corpses. They left a lingering shadow on her, a mark. And now she couldn't go back to Jerome and decompress. But she knew it would be impossible for her to say no, not if it helped a child find her way home, dead or alive. She followed Mike back into the chilly morgue. Soon he was pulling open body drawers, citing the Tanner stages—the ages of sexual development—of the girls as he went. Most were Tanner stage four: about thirteen or fourteen. One was barely pubescent. Her narrow, undeveloped body reminded Naomi of the street girl she had confronted outside the library. Celia, she remembered.

Part of her licensing as an investigator was in examining remains, but Naomi's greatest knowledge came from her past. She put the last foot back down on the table. For a long moment she stood motionless. She was remembering how after running in escape, her feet had hurt for weeks. The ground had been too tender to touch, so Naomi had wrapped her feet in Mrs. Cottle's flowered dishcloths and hobbled around until her soles toughened.

Once free, Naomi couldn't stop moving. Mrs. Cottle had understood. It was a puzzle because Naomi had never asked Mrs. Cottle *how* she knew, and now it was too late. Naomi had run away, as usual. She had an excuse—she was working a missing child case at the time—but she had missed saying good-bye to the only mother she had ever known.

"They weren't in the river very long, but I bet you knew that. A day or two at most," Naomi said. "What needs to be investigated is what happened before the murders."

Mike stepped closer. "What do you mean, what happened before?"

Naomi lifted the white foot. "Look at these feet. No calluses. None of them have any signs of wear or activity on their feet. It's one of the first signs you see in cases of captivity."

"Jerome?"

He was sitting in Diane's living room, ensconced in her velvet sofa. The room had the scent of incense and the leftover pizza he had heated for lunch.

He looked up, his face cautious.

"I'm sorry." She went to him, sat down, held on. She felt his hair against her cheek. She had always loved his hair. Naomi knew that might not be the right way to see it—Jerome was Kalapuya, an Oregon native—but those childhood memories, of magic, held on. For her, at least.

"I'm tired of moving, Naomi." She saw his firm mouth, the tender chin. "I'm tired of being second best."

"You're not—"

"Yes, I am. Either we make this a partnership or it doesn't work."

Naomi felt fear. It was a fear as vast as an empty tomorrow. "What does that mean?" she asked.

"We need to put down roots. Make a home, someplace. It doesn't have to be forever, but it needs to be now."

"I need to find my sister."

"I know." His voice was gentle.

That broke her. She wept against him, just as she had cried against Diane, and he put his arm around her. It wasn't just fear of not finding her sister, Naomi realized. It was fear she would not be strong enough to stay once she did.

* * *

When Jerome was little, a woman came for him. She came picking her way over a yard littered with dog turds, swollen black garbage bags, a knocked-over hibachi with a vacant grill. The woman had the look of a farmhouse wife, the kind of grandma you see in books. She wore a checkered or flowered dress—now he wasn't sure—stout shoes, the kind of thick pantyhose you wear for varicose veins. Her hair was silver and piled on her head, and her eyes were a kind, bright, merry blue that said Christmas and cookies rolled into one.

Angrily, his last foster family shoved his belongings—another black garbage bag, this one full of torn shirts and a broken frame photo of his mom, who had died when he was an infant—out the door. Later, back on the farmhouse porch, Mrs. Cottle carefully took everything out and even folded the garbage bag into a tiny square. "When you have lost everything, everything matters," she had said, in her gentle voice. "I will keep this for you."

But before that, she had called him out of the weeds at the edge of that other yard, a skinny little boy with arms covered with painful deerfly bites. Mrs. Cottle had taken him by the hand and led him to her truck. They had driven away, forever. Jerome had looked up at her, riding tall behind the wheel, and she had looked down at him and smiled.

"You're going to be okay," she had said, with the sure conviction of any mother. "I'll see to that."

And she had.

Mrs. Cottle had said the exact same thing to Naomi, too, when she arrived. Jerome wondered if Naomi even remembered it. She acted like she had forgotten what it was like to be found. Jerome, who had found refuge in family, did not understand why Naomi kept running. She had found safety before, and had it now. But still—she ran.

Celia had been on the street, what now, six, seven months? She counted, dispirited, the butterfly book blurry in front of her.

Nine months. It had been nine months.

She would turn thirteen soon. A birthday on the streets—she had seen those. Street kids trying to pretend that going into the soup kitchen and trying to find a candle to stick in a pile of beans was okay. No. Not for her. It would be better to spend her birthdays in the library, drawing as rain ran down the windows, and the afternoons passed into nights, and the seasons passed into years, and one day soon she would find her feet on the stone stairs outside, years older.

She had no future. She knew that.

"You can become an electrician." The street kids were playing the game of what-if. "I saw an ad about that once. All you need is your diploma."

"I'm going to be an airline pilot."

"Naw! That's fucking bullshit, man."

"Really."

"You need like eight thousand degrees. My mom dated this guy once, he was a pilot—"

"Your mom sucked cock down here with the rest, Stoner."

The voices faded out. Celia was sitting on the curb with the others. She was aware night was coming. The sunset had lit the sky above them into tatters of orange and blood red, streaks of lavender and a bruised purple like a kiss. The city buildings rose like giant smiles, and in each window Celia saw an eye. The figures moving inside, turning off lights and lowering shades, reassured her.

Rich plopped down next to her. His broad, sweaty face looked at her with concern. "You've been quiet lately." He suddenly sounded much older, and Celia could see him as a boyfriend, a man, to some future woman.

"I'm turning thirteen soon," she said, reaching forward and capturing her toes. They were starting to poke through her canvas shoes.

"Really? That's cool." But Rich knew. His measured glance told her.

"You really think you're ever getting off the streets, Rich?" she asked.

She saw the crumbs in his eyes, the dirt on his forehead, the curly hair starting under his chin. The beginnings of a mustache. The pink line of his lips, the uncertain eyes, and for the first time she wondered about his past. What had made Rich? He was as gentle as a butterfly.

"Sometimes I think I'll get off the streets, get a job," he said. He picked a bottle cap out of the gutter. "But I don't think they make jobs for people like us. I mean, me. What would I tell them?" His voice was forlorn.

Celia had no answer. She looked at the sky, unfurling like glorious banners. All through the world people shared this sky. They didn't know she deserved a piece, too.

*   *   *

Oh, the butterflies. It was like a chant. Once Celia had passed a shop up in a tony highbrow neighborhood called Pearl or something equally stupid. What had her mom once said? "It doesn't matter what color you paint a turd, it's still a turd." The shop had said MAGIC in the window, and SPELLS, and Celia had been intrigued. But when she went inside and tried to smell the incense that cost ten dollars or look at the glass balls that turned out to be plastic, the woman clerk had made an expression that told Celia she was the painted turd and should leave.

Celia had stood outside for a long time, then, thinking about magic and spells, just as she was now, getting ever more lost inside herself, only it wasn't lost; she was *finding* herself, someplace deep in this warren of memories. She was tracing her steps *back*. To the beginning.

It was her most precious memory. She was very young, maybe three. She was with her mother in a sunny meadow. It was the time of sweetness, before Teddy. Her mother had her hands clasped over Celia's eyes. Counting, each breath like a measured, small bell. One, two.

Three.

"Look, Celia!"

She had opened her eyes, let the bright in. Focus.

Oh.

They were bright as discs of color, circling like the spots of sun. A blue brighter than the sky, a sunshine yellow tipped with gold coming closer.

"Butterflies!"

The butterflies would always be there, Celia thought now, feeling her bottom against the curb, the faint voices of the other street kids, the gassy smell of exhaust growing distant. Walking hand in hand with her mother through the meadow, she saw one land on a purple flower.

"What's this one, Momma?"

"A great spangled fritillary."

Her mother had picked a dandelion and rubbed it under Celia's chin, laughing, but the yellow petals were no match for the yellow of the golden butterflies. The white of an eye could not be whiter than the butterfly whites, and no sky was a match for their iridescent blues. Celia, like her mother, was in a swoon.

Tiny feckless feet on burred limbs. Kind eyes that rotated, seeing all. Even Celia. Celia was not a monster that day.

"Where you going, Momma?"

"Time to go, sweetie."

Celia had wanted her mother to stay—she had grabbed her hand. Now, sitting on the curb, her face slack with memory, Celia was unaware that her own hand was wide open and reaching out.

Her mother's eyes had softened. She had smiled.

"Okay. Let me tell you a story, then, about the most magical place of all. It's called the butterfly museum."

*   *   *

The scar-faced man. He had begun to haunt Celia's life. She saw him on the corners, melting into the crowd. He was in the corner market, picking through the sandwiches as she and her friends reached for the marked-down cartons of milk, the ones they had to sniff carefully before drinking. Once at the river, he was watching the bridge as she and the boys crossed—that really freaked her out. "Did you see him? Did you see him?" she kept asking the others.

Now he was staring at her from down the street. He frowned at her, the scars on his lips wriggling like little worms. Celia pointed him out to the others.

"He's a perp." Stoner laughed, and Celia knew then that the boys really weren't going to keep her safe. They had no idea what it was like to be a girl.

"I think he's trying to kill me," Celia said, with fearful simplicity.

"Float you in the river with so many holes you might drown?" said another street girl who came up to Celia, her hair a bright orange flood in the dusk.

"Would you want that?" Celia asked her, a girl she had never seen before. Kids came and went: trains, buses, hitchhiking. Many ended up captives, pure and simple, kept like dogs in dirty hotel rooms.

The girl shrugged. She had pimples on her chin, small fleshy eyes, earlobes like globes of fat. She smiled at Celia, showing a line of mercury teeth. "Anything is better than this," the girl said, sashaying away, her hips pounding a beat only Celia could hear.

And then there was the woman. The one with the glossy tail of hair. Galloping up and down the street, sticking her flyers on telephone poles. Celia saw her and sighed. The woman took whatever fun there was out of the night.

The women's shelter was called Aspire. The sign was bolted on the side of a building that had seen better days. Pigeons, roosting, had left the brick sides a smeary Jackson Pollock painting of bird droppings. Inside was a familiar sad smell: sweat, sorrow, grief. Naomi passed a large dorm room, empty and waiting for nightfall, the cots tucked hard with green army blankets. A sign-up clipboard for available bunks hung to the side of the door. The last bunk for the night had been claimed by a woman named Laverne.

In the dayroom Naomi found a table of women playing cards. Whist, from the look of it. One was the skinny bald woman she had seen before, digging through the gutter. She seemed to be in a much better place today, sitting upright, dealing a card. A heavy-set woman was at the head of the game, wearing an Aspire shirt. "Game's full, honey."

Naomi showed her license, explaining her cause.

"I seen your flyers around," the woman said, dealing another card. "Would have called you if I knew, but there's not much there. Twenty-five, white? It could be anyone."

The other women nodded, sagely. All looked to be in their forties or older and hard-bitten. Naomi told them her story, emphasizing how she was checking to see if her sister had ended up in the city.

"I don't know anyone who talked a story like that," the woman said, taking a drag on a cigarette and putting it down in an overflowing ashtray. "You say you were held in some bunker out in the woods?"

"I've heard shit like that, even worse," the older bald woman said, serenely.

"Really?" Naomi turned to her. "Like what?"

"Yeah, what?" another woman asked.

"Right here, in this town. Shit you wouldn't believe. Maybe you would, stay on the streets long enough."

"Amen right there, sure enough," one of the women said, reaching for a card.

The bald woman looked at her hand. "I heard some creep is taking those girls. Keeps them in some house, cuts them to pieces."

Naomi felt her heart pound. "How do you know that?"

"Men talk. Maybe they smell it on each other. Dogs."

"Yeah, uh-huh," another woman agreed, picking up the communal cigarette and adding her own lipstick stain.

"Do you know where this house is?"

"Hell no. You think I want to get my ass anywhere near such craziness? I got enough troubles as it is. Besides, I'm too old for him to take. Thank the Lord."

None of the women seemed fazed. One shook her head, passing a card.

"Who might know more?" Naomi asked.

"Maybe those little kids he's taking." Another drag on the smoke. "Poor babies."

Naomi pulled up a chair. "Help me," she said, smiling.

The women exchanged looks, laughed. They talked with Naomi until the shelter manager stubbed out her final smoke and said the fun was over, it was time to turn down the beds. Turning down the beds, Naomi found out, meant checking in the long line of women who had appeared outside. No weapons, no pets, no drugs. There was a line of battered lockers for locking up the knives, sharpened screwdrivers, and other self-defense tools the women carried.

Naomi followed, helping as best she could. "I'm curious about a man I've seen around," she said, describing the scar-faced man.

"Oh, I've seen him," the manager said, pulling a stack of the olive green army blankets out of a locker and handing it to a short woman behind her, beaten by time.

"You have?" Naomi asked.

"Sure. Major creep if you ask me. Seen him loitering around. There's not much we can do about the pimps and rapists hanging outside. Scratch that. There's *nothing* we can do."

In the dorm room women were milling around and sitting on the edges of their beds. One of the volunteers who had been playing cards circulated with tiny paper cups of juice and packets of donated cookies. Baskets of high-demand items—sanitary napkins and face wipes—sat on tables at the edges of the room. *One per day*, handwritten signs said. The women seemed relaxed, as if the stress of the streets was rising off their shoulders.

"You come back, in the morning," the manager said, shutting the locker. "We unlock the doors then and the women leave. Ten dollars you'll see some pimp in a car, thinking he can grab the woman he was beating and get her back in the fold. Or you go outside right now, when the women line up. It's like open season out there." There was bitterness and hurt in her voice. "That's why we lock the doors every night. To keep us safe. Lord help me, though, sometimes I want to go out there and give them payback. But then I'd be the one in jail. I got a friend doing life for killing her pimp."

Naomi thought of the river, wide and deep. She thought of the girl she had seen pulled out by the bridge. "If there was a place close by where someone wanted to throw a body in the river and not be seen, where would it be?" she asked.

"The industrial area, at the old docks," the woman answered immediately. She smiled at Naomi. "I grew up here. I was an honor student, back in my day." The smile vanished. "Then one of those pimps caught me. Made me feel loved for the first time, and it was all a lie."

"One more question—"

"Time for me to lock the doors, honey." Behind them in the dorm the women were laughing. One had put a pillowcase on her shoulders as some sort of cape and was telling a story.

"There are children out there. Aren't there any shelters for them?" Naomi's voice was pleading.

The manager stopped. She shook her head.

"Why not?" Naomi asked.

"I think it's a legal thing," the woman answered. "The city would be responsible. There's some shelters for older youth. But not for the younger ones. Little kids, why, they leave the shelter and get killed or raped, the city's got a lawsuit on their hands. Easier to just pretend they don't exist." She paused. "Maybe we're afraid to admit they're there. What that says about us."

"I appreciate what you do," Naomi said, somberly.

The woman looked surprised. "I appreciate you, too, honey."

Naomi stepped outside, hearing the door close for the night behind her. In the distance she heard a bird. Finch, she thought automatically. Even here. It made her long for the clean crispness of a farm field at dawn, or the trail through the woods you know will loop and return to safety. But she could smell the river, and was struck for the first time that the city, too, had its own beauty.

Down the street, a group of street kids had gathered in the dusk. The little girl Naomi had run to save by the library was sitting among them, the big boy next to her.

Here she comes," Rich said, and one of the other kids picked it up into song: "Miss America . . ."

"Her tits ain't big enough," Stoner said.

"Ha! Caught you looking," Rich answered.

"She's better-looking than that creepy guy Celia keeps seeing, the one with the scars."

The kids fell silent as the woman approached. To Celia, sitting at the curb, Naomi looked tall enough to touch the stars. Her shiny head was Orion, sparkling in the sky. At least she had made the scar-faced man disappear. He had vanished from the corner.

"Well, hello!" She smiled at everyone.

Celia looked at her nice shoes. They were leather and laced up the front, with low walking soles. Thick. Comfortable-looking. Celia spit on the sidewalk, close enough to those shoes to make a point.

"Fuck, Celia, that's harsh," Rich said. He stood up, smiling at the pretty woman. "That's no way to treat someone." Celia turned away. "I'm sorry for my friend here," Rich said.

Celia made a small noise of contempt. Her face felt hot with embarrassment. All the other kids were looking at her like she was an asshole.

"I'm looking for my sister," Naomi was telling the others.

"We saw the flyers," Stoner offered.

Celia's eyes secretly traveled up the trousers, past the sturdy middle, saw the underside of her soft chin, the planes of her face. So this was the woman who had written the flyer in the annex of Sisters of Mercy. *Tell her I am sorry*, the flyer had said. *I miss her.*

The street kids looked at one another, shrugged. No one knew anything.

"Don't know a thing. I'd tell you if I did," Rich offered, gallantly. "No one should lose their sister."

Celia got up, walked away.

Celia walked until she found herself at the church at the top of downtown. The evening bells were ringing. The streets looked clean, swept by the rain brooms of God. Celia had been to no kind of church, ever, except for the one that mattered, and that was the church of the butterflies.

They flew around her, even now. Butterflies are emissaries of God, her mother had said, that fateful day before the flood of darkness came over them both. Every country has butterflies, she had said. There is no place you can go without butterflies.

"Not even the deserts, Momma?"

"Not even. The sagebrush checkerspot lives there."

"You know a lot about butterflies, Momma."

"I wanted to be a lepidopterist, when I was young."

"What happened, Momma?"

No answer, the words taken by time. But Celia could swear that she had learned about butterflies deep within her mother's womb. Her mother had fed them to Celia with her own blood, and when she was born, the sack was pulsating with them, so the doctor stood back, astounded as she erupted, covered with wings.

Those butterflies had flown away, but Celia knew. They were emissaries of God.

She climbed the steps of the church, and a man stood at the top, smiling at her. He handed her a pamphlet, though Celia probably stank. Inside most of the pews were empty. At the booths on the side, Celia was told, she could confess. But Celia didn't want God to forgive her. She wanted life to forgive her, and she didn't even know why. She walked deeper into the church and smelled the old incense, the warm cloth of people. Their skins, their hopes, their sins. She looked up to the altar and asked the white figure on the cross, Did God bring butterflies to you, too? Did your mother hold her hands over your eyes, and count, and whisper?

When Celia got back, Naomi was gone. No one talked about her. It was as if she didn't exist. The day people were like that. If this was hell, they were in heaven, and they peeked around the clouds to look down at the others, then flew away like unconcerned angels.

She found Stoner and Rich in the dumpster behind the Greek restaurant. The tall girl with the phone told her where to look. The owner of the Greek restaurant refused to spray his dumpster with

Raid or pour bleach on the food. The business association was trying to make him, but the old man said no, his people knew what it was to go hungry.

Unfortunately, everyone else knew about the dumpster, so usually it was picked over. But tonight, Stoner had found a foil tray of crusty moussaka, and this he was eating by the palmful. Rich nuzzled from an empty yogurt container. He had been licking it, and there was now white yogurt under his chin. Celia didn't say what it looked like. The world was gross, sometimes.

"Hey, let me," Celia bossed, and Stoner passed her the tray. Celia scooped a piece out with her dirty fingers, ate. It tasted really good. She bet it would taste even better heated up. Once a month at school lunch, they'd had international day, and the food had tasted this good.

In the alley entryway a bum appeared, shambling like a scarecrow. The street kids gave him the eye. He gave them the finger in return but left. First come, first served was street law. The street people were hungry for rules, thought Celia, maybe because the rest of their lives were so lawless. Sometimes the older kids formed hard-edged street families with laws of their own. Celia stayed away. She'd had enough law to last her a lifetime.

The streetlights flickered. It was getting too dark to see. Their shifting feet made crunching sounds in the alley. Stoner and Rich and Celia ate the moussaka until it was all gone and their bellies hurt. It made Celia think of how caterpillars can eat two hundred times their own weight. That was Celia, eating until her thorax expanded.

Celia had once heard a story of a girl who escaped the streets and gained so much weight she couldn't move. Celia thought maybe that was one of those made-up stories. But it made sense to her. If she had all the food in the world, she might eat it, too. But unlike that girl she would eventually stop, put her arms over her own face, curl into a ball, and rest until spring, when she could be born anew.

Naomi, having barely made up with Jerome, felt she was sliding on an ice cap that ended at his shoulder. She woke in the same bed with him, but though they lay close together, there was a distance that had never been there before.

Rising quietly so as to not awaken him, she considered her conviction that her sister was alive. But how could she know that if she couldn't even remember her name? Her mind skittered uncomfortably away from this thought.

It was very early. Outside, the birds were quiet. The dark sky lay over the city like a silent blanket. Naomi wondered where Celia and the other street kids slept at night.

* * *

Naomi met Sean Richardson from the Feds in a café on the first floor of his building. He had called asking to see her. From their table Naomi watched the businesspeople pass, always in a hurry.

She thought of the homeless on skid row, only blocks away and yet in a completely different world.

"Are you always so quiet?" Richardson asked, sipping his coffee. "I had always heard you were super friendly. Big smile and all."

"The past year took it out of me," Naomi admitted.

Richardson noted the ring on her finger, didn't say anything. His own hand was as lonely as his heart. Some people didn't know how lucky they were. "I got a call from the medical examiner," he said. "He told me in a few minutes of examination you were able to pick up something neither he nor my team noticed."

Naomi took another sip of her coffee.

"Their feet were soft," she explained. "Even children show wear on their feet from daily use. Corns, calluses, broken nails. None of those girls had walked for weeks."

His brown eyes looked pained. "Anything else?"

Naomi paused for only a moment. She decided to take a risk. "I heard about a house where the girls might be kept before they are killed. I don't know where it is—yet."

Outside the crowds were dwindling. Everyone had scurried inside the buildings where they worked, which Naomi now imagined as giant hives, the workers nesting bees.

"And you?" Naomi asked. "Has your man on the ground found anything?"

He shook his head. "I'm thinking of hiring one of those profilers."

"You guys really don't learn, do you?"

He flushed. His brown eyes were on her. "Do you think this has something to do with your sister? All this time?"

Naomi was staring at him, as if he were a grim reaper.

"Breakfast?" Naomi stuck her head in Winfield's door.

They went to his favorite deli at the top of downtown. The food was crap, but the waitresses comped Winfield's meals. Naomi noticed a group of street kids in one booth—Celia was not among them—and wondered how long such kids had been in plain sight and she had not noticed them. Winfield ordered a Denver omelet while Naomi asked for a tofu scramble.

His eyebrows went up at that. "Didn't know you for a tofu gal."

"I'm trying something new, spark my appetite."

Winfield added three sugars to his coffee, looked over his cup. The Naomi he had known had the appetite of a truck driver.

"This city is a hell of a mess," Naomi said after the food arrived and she took a small, curious bite. They were in Winfield's favorite booth, the window shielded, easy access to both the front and back doors. Winfield was safety conscious like that. When he walked with her down the street, he ambled at her side like a bear. She thought it was silly. What could he protect her from?

Winfield shook hot sauce over his omelet. "You must be hanging out on skid row."

"It isn't a row anymore, it's a mile," Naomi said. She explained what the woman at Aspire had said about the lack of shelters for children. Her eyes kept glancing at the street kids as she spoke.

"That what you want to talk about?" Winfield said, scooping

food into his mouth and quickly wiping. The Naomi he knew also didn't waste time on what she couldn't fix. She kept her eye on the prize. Naomi reminded Winfield of the parable of the starfish: A man, out on the beach one day, stopped to find a boy throwing starfish back into the sea. There were hundreds of starfish washed up on the beach, and the man explained to the boy he couldn't save them all. "I can save one," the boy replied.

"I want to know if my sister is in the state mental hospital," Naomi said. "It would explain why I can't find her."

Winfield wanted to point out that maybe Naomi couldn't find her sister because she didn't even know her name. But Winfield knew this was how investigations were solved, one small step at a time. "I can call down there for you, ask," he said.

"I'd rather visit in person. Can you get me clearance? It takes longer if I try."

"Sure." Like a lot of cops, Winfield ate like there was a timer in the room. Naomi once used to beat him to the bell, but not anymore. She pushed her plate aside.

"Not good?"

"Just not very hungry lately."

Yes, something was wrong with Naomi. The waitress came to take their plates. She smiled. Winfield put down some dollar bills for a tip.

"Something else bothering you, child finder?" he asked, rising heavily.

"Just the usual," Naomi replied sardonically. Her sister was missing. Wasn't that enough?

"The world is full of heartache," the detective said. Naomi could see the sadness he bore, too. "You got to carve out some happiness for yourself. Otherwise it will take you down."

Naomi nodded, looking away.

"Saw your husband the other day," Winfield added as they headed out. He held the heavy door open for her, eyes scanning the street.

"Where?"

"Down at the licensing agency. He was asking after being an investigator, like you."

He saw her face. She hadn't known.

Naomi found a note from Jerome on the kitchen counter. Raised in the country without cell service, they had the habit of leaving notes for each other instead of sending text messages.

Gone to the firing range, the note said. Jerome's truck—adapted for driving with one arm—was gone from outside, and the house was empty. Walking heavily up the narrow stairs to their guest room, she saw his holster was no longer over the chair.

Carrying a gun never worked for Naomi. Whenever she wore one, her leads dried up, and witnesses refused to talk. She could swear people could smell it on her. For her a gun was a small object that fired wildly, threatened fewer than it should, silenced the good witnesses and emboldened the bad. She preferred to use her hands. She had extensive self-defense training and stayed in good shape. She had had some close calls, but so far it had worked.

Sitting at the end of the bed, Naomi looked around the room. She remembered the times over the years she had shown up here, exhausted from travel, and Diane had taken her in, let her spend a night or two, and hugged her wordlessly when she left. Here was where Naomi had left her heart. The walls were covered with cards sent by the families of children she had saved. Thank-you notes and *How are you doing, child finder?* Concern in their voices for her. The kids could always tell. She remembered the soft touch of one girl, looking up at her and *knowing*.

"I hope you don't get lost," the girl had said.

Lost. You can be lost even when you've been found. You can make the wrong turn in life even if you're surrounded by people who love you. That was what suicide was, Naomi figured. It was choosing the final exit instead of another path. Not because you wanted to hurt anyone, but because you feel too hopeless to find your way home. There was more than one kind of suicide, too, more than one kind of leaving. How many people spend their entire lives not even knowing that they have already left?

She leaned over, sighing. Diane and Jerome were right. The past year she had stopped even thinking about anyone else. All she had cared about was finding her sister. When Jerome came back, they would talk about their future. She would tell him she thought it was a good idea for him to get his investigator license. He could help her, and still make some money on his own cases.

And they would talk about her stopping running, at least for the time.

* * *

Diane spent her days saying good-bye to the past. She figured this was what lonely people did, and since she had done everything in her life with gusto—from being a short-order cook to put herself through college to running a treatment center for emotionally disturbed teenagers—she had decided to do lonely well, too.

She went to the train station with the clock tower and ordered a cosmopolitan in the adjoining jazz lounge, which looked unchanged since the '40s. That was in memory of her dear mother, who had once nurtured a dream of being a jazz singer but instead became a pediatrician. She went to the Chinese gardens where she had met her first and only love, a woman named Marsha. Then she drove into the west hills to visit the Japanese gardens, where they had watched the koi on the day when Marsha told her that she was going to die. That had been over twenty years before, she reflected now. On the way down she stopped at the high concrete aqueduct known as the suicide bridge, the site of one of her greatest regrets. There a teenage patient named Daniel had swan-dived to his death.

But getting back in her car Diane realized she was being silly. This wasn't how she wanted to spend her final years—being alone. There would be enough loneliness after death, she figured. She would go home and tell Naomi that she wanted her, and Jerome, to stay. They could make a family. It wouldn't be the most ordinary family, but it was something.

Diane turned her key in the door. Jerome and Naomi sat close together on the couch, waiting for her. Naomi was trembling, ever so slightly. Diane could see it in the hand holding the teapot.

A cup was waiting for her.

◂

"That wasn't what I expected," Diane told her evening mirror, later. She could see the fine crepe under her eyes. She picked up the hairbrush on the vanity. She seldom used it: it had been her mother's. She inspected a strand of silver hair in it, wondering if it was hers.

She remembered the last days of Marsha's death from liver cancer, when she had become delirious, breaking vases, trying to attack Diane. The hospice nurses had to wrap her hands in thick mittens to keep her from clawing out her own eyes. Marsha had died right here, in this house, in a hospital cot set up in the living room. Diane had never regretted it. It was a precious thing, to say an intimate good-bye.

"We want to stay here, with you, if you will have us," Naomi had said, and Diane had seen the flutter in her throat, and how Jerome had turned to look at his wife as if a miracle had happened.

The librarian kept stacks of scrap paper—soft pink, yellow, plain white—in a small wood box on her desk next to a cup of stubby pencils. Celia took a handful of the paper, looking at the librarian to see if it was too much, but the woman only smiled. Celia carried the paper and pencil and her favorite book to her favorite chair, upstairs in the big room, where the light came in the windows no matter how hard it rained.

Most of the time she drew butterflies—long, magical butterflies, with trailing wings and otherwordly eyes. But other times she drew her sister, tracing her face as if to remember it always. When Celia drew her sister, or anyone she loved, she added butterflies: all over their shoulders, sprouting from their eyebrows. Even the tiny dot inside the eye became a single, precious beast. In this way the butterflies were the people she loved and the people she loved were free.

When she was done with the drawings, Celia slid them into her favorite book. It was the only safe place she knew to keep them. They would get wet under the overpass and lost on the streets.

Celia knew it was hard to find safe places. The most unsafe places were the cars and the beds of any man. Alleys and dark tunnels. Any place where she could be trapped. The secret to survival was a map inside her mind, where Celia was always trying, like a butterfly, to find the right place to land. But there seemed to be no such place.

It was cold under the overpass when Celia awoke the next morning, and she felt a stinging sensation on her leg. She lifted her jeans to see a large, raised red spider bite. She knew it was a spider because the insect had gotten squished against the cloth. Probably she had rolled on it when it bit her.

"Is this a black widow?" Celia asked, pulling the jean cloth inside out.

"Looks like a black smear to me," Stoner said. Rich peered closer. All of them had seen street kids with bad wounds from infected rat and insect bites. Celia vividly remembered one girl who got a cockroach stuck in her ear while sleeping in an abandoned house. Her screaming carried for blocks.

"I hear you can bathe in bleach and it kills germs," Stoner said.

"You say that all the time," Celia said.

"Well, it's true. You just have to dilute it."

"I don't have a bathtub."

"I guess you could do it in the river."

Celia and Rich looked at Stoner like he was insane. He blushed. He bit his thick lips, looked away, hoped they would drop it. They did. Celia limped to standing. Maybe if she walked it off the pain would go away.

"I'll go with you to the free clinic," Rich offered.

The free clinic was at the top of skid row, along the park blocks where the city police were always tearing down the tents the homeless families put up. Celia and Rich sat on the slashed seats for hours, waiting to be seen. The doctors there were nice, but did it matter?

Her stomach felt like a cave, and she was dizzy from hunger when she finally got called back to the exam room. For some reason she kept thinking of peanuts, and the salty taste flooded her mouth at the thought of one. If she had a peanut, she would suck on it for like an hour.

Celia had been in the free clinic before. That had been for an STD check. Celia didn't want to get pregnant or get STDs. She was worried about her period starting because then it would mean she could have a baby, and she already had one—her sister. She had told the doctor all this while filling her pockets with the free condoms, not understanding why his face looked so sad.

Day people.

The doctor was a tall, skinny man with black curly hair, like Stoner grown up, only with a small round potbelly under his white jacket, which already had smears and stains from other patients. He smelled like Juicy Fruit gum. He looked at Celia's leg, at the red raised circle around the spider bite and the hole in the middle. She showed him the dead squished spider. "I left it there so you could see it," she said proudly.

She read his name tag as he leaned over. DR. ALEX LOPEZ, it said, and she thought of the scar-faced man and his nameless blue jacket.

"Well, I don't think it's a recluse or widow," he said doubtfully, looking at the squished bug. He cleaned the bite and wrapped it with a clean bandage that would be filthy or lost within a day. He shook his head as she left, knowing he would make the mandated report call, and the recording about yet another homeless child on the streets would enter whatever endless system stored them, for a caseworker to find next week or next month. Even when they picked the kids up, they had nowhere to take them. The doctor had heard about kids sleeping in child welfare offices, on the floor.

Outside, the rain had started again. Rich was waiting for her, so hungry, too, that he felt faint. Together they walked down to skid row, looking for food and their friends. Celia wondered if butterflies savor time more because they know they will die soon. Then again, Celia knew she might die soon, too, and that didn't make her enjoy life more.

"I saw a doctor who looked like you," Celia told Stoner, importantly. Rich had panhandled enough money to buy them both sandwiches from the corner market, and Celia had finished hers. She kept the crumpled paper in her pocket, touching it for reassurance that she had eaten.

"Yeah?" Stoner wasn't paying attention. He was panhandling on the corner, almost coming out of his skin with worry. Anxiety, Celia guessed. ADH-motherfucking-D. Jostling, dancing, his long legs so skinny they never met.

"Except he had like a beer belly."

Stoner snorted. "I'll never have one of those."

"I bet you're related."

"Why?" She had his attention now. His dreamy eyes, thick with lashes, met hers. Stoner was a pretty boy. The men in the cars said that all the time. But he was pretty in a way that wasn't just for perverts. He had those beautiful eyes, curly black hair, and golden skin. Stoner was part Puerto Rican. Puerto Ricans, he said, cross the street for each other.

"His name was Lopez. What's your name?"

Stoner was staring at her. "Don't be an idiot, Celia," he said.

"Why not?" she persisted.

"We're not all related, okay?"

"Fine." Celia stared at the cars. Another old man gestured at her, twinkling his fingers like a fucking creep. Ignoring him, she tried to panhandle, but no one wanted to give her any money. It was always that way trying to beg as a girl. The men in suits hurried away like they were afraid to be seen talking to the merchandise. The women walked faster when she approached, like she was a disease they might carry home to their daughters. You'd think the day people would give more to the street girls, but it didn't happen that way.

* * *

Every Friday in school, Celia was pulled out of class early. She held a ruler out and whacked the lockers as she passed. The kids weren't allowed to use the lockers anymore. It wasn't safe, the principal said.

She would sit in the waiting chairs with the others. There were always three or so of them. Kids on lice check. The nurse was a rude lady named Sally who blew out her nasty breath in frustration whenever she checked Celia. First she checked Celia's head for lice, then her arms for the ringworm that kept growing in circular patches, and, finally, her wrists and legs for the angry, scratched red trails of scabies.

Your child has ____, the form note said, and the nurse would fill in the bug of the month for Celia to carry home. *Please treat your child before returning him/her to school.*

"Just give me the medicine," Celia started telling the nurse, who refused. Finally it was Mrs. Wilkerson who did, sneaking it to Celia like it was some sort of contraband. She locked herself in their bathroom at home while her mom slept on the couch and rubbed the foul pink pesticides all over her naked body and scalp until she was covered in the sticky mess. She waited, head down, shivering, not thinking while the medicine worked, and then she stepped into the dirty tub and rinsed off with the old yogurt container left at the side.

Sometimes, when Celia was hungry, she would eat the plaster chunks that fell from her bedroom wall. They tasted sweet. The paint from the windowsills also tasted sweet, but Mrs. Wilkerson had told the kids not to eat the paint in their homes because it had lead in it.

Celia often dreamed of the day her mother would stop using. She would walk into the house. Her mother would look up, her face clear and bright. She would smile, and her eyes would be determined. We're leaving Teddy, she would say happily. Tell your sister.

*   *   *

Munch, munch, like the sky ate the moon every night, until only a sliver remained. Like Stoner standing at the edge of the street, searching for every tablet and drop, talking about liquid acid you put in your eyes, or sticky stuff to melt into the brown liquid that made your soul flow down the streets. All that begging and hustling only to get some fix he would forget tomorrow.

Only Celia and Rich remained clean, sitting on the corner while the night spiraled out of control around them. It wasn't out of some snotty judgment or anything like that, but more a matter of laziness or fear. If someone had come up to Celia and said, *Here*, she might have, despite all her promises to herself. At some point the night would be right. Then she would be like one of the junkies on the streets whose veins had all collapsed into dry little threads.

It made Celia think of how butterflies turn poison into protection. The monarch eats milkweed plants and turns them into honest-to-God cyanide, so any predator that eats it will die. Celia liked that. She wished she was capable of killing men for just a taste. She imagined what the streets would look like then. But the poison comes with a cost, she thought. The butterfly, eaten, still dies.

Naomi drove into the industrial area the Aspire manager had mentioned, finding the deserted waterfront that ran next to skid row. She parked her car and walked to the edge of the decaying docks. From here she could look downriver and see the city.

It would be easy to throw a body into the river here, unseen. It would take a day or so for it to resurface, down by the bridge. It lined up.

Naomi stepped tentatively onto one of the docks. The wood was splintered, the creosote-soaked pilings mired deep in the muddy water. Feeling each board carefully, Naomi made her way out to the pier. The water sloshed over the edges of the rotting wood. She could feel how deep the river ran underneath. The channel was big and dark ahead of her.

She walked to the end of the dock and peered down into murky depths. Tangles of old rebar, sprouting like lethal rusted spears, rose from the unseen bottom. Anyone who fell over the side here was courting death, or at least a trip to the emergency room and a tetanus shot.

Naomi imagined a man carrying a body. She saw him coming out here in the dark, with only the moonlight for illumination. He carried the body to the dock and dumped it off the edge, certain the river would erase any evidence from the corpse and the current would carry it far enough away no one would know where it had been dumped.

Getting down on her hands and knees on the wet boards, Naomi examined both sides of the dock. She took her time, crawling, peering at the underboards, studying the oily pilings. More nests of the rebar rose from the gloomy depths below, like lazy venomous snakes. She assumed the rebar was from the shipping industry that once made this city—coils of shipping cables and reinforcement for pilings that had since rotted away.

She froze. There was a pale reddish glint on the end of one of the spears. It was about a foot beneath the surface, waving like the softest filaments, or mermaid floss. Pushing up her sleeve, Naomi lay down flat on the wet boards. The shockingly cold water wet her arm. She reached down for the floss, brought it to the surface with her fingers.

It was a hank of human hair.

Back on the relief of dry land, Naomi stood in the rutted dirt and pulled out her phone, ignoring the cold water running down her sleeve.

"Sean Richardson?" she asked. "You need to bring a team down to the old docks. Yes. In the industrial area adjacent to downtown.

A dredge team, with divers experienced with river hazards. You are going to find more missing girls here. They're snagged."

She stayed only long enough to see the cars and dark vans arrive. The search and rescue boat came down the river, the divers holding on to the sides. A news copter drew a bead in the distance, but Naomi left before anyone tried to talk to her.

If Jerome had the firing range, Naomi had the boxing gym. The best was when she had real people to spar with—it seemed every town offered up at least a few curious longshoremen, teenage martial arts hopefuls, or retired prizefighters willing to go a few rounds. If she ever did settle in one place, Naomi figured, she might take a few girls under her arm to train.

She found the local gym on the east side of town, near a set of train tracks and a disreputable strip of car lots. The smell was intoxicating: sweat, old leather, and the musky scent of fear. To Naomi, new fear smelled bright and hard, but fear already spent smelled entirely different, like an animal resting.

The young men—and more women, she noticed—had faces lacquered with Vaseline. The only language was the hiss of breath and the smack of the bags, and gloves hitting flesh. Naomi spoke to the woman in charge, a retired female fighter, one of the first, of pink shorts and a bannered name. Now she was just smiling, ruddy faced, a team of kids around her.

Naomi changed in a tiny bathroom where the sink was stained with spit blood, and carried her boxing bag back out by the ring that dominated the room. She warmed up, shadowboxing and hitting the heavy bags while the others snuck glances, curious about her. Then she wrapped her hands, asked the trainer to help lace her sparring gloves, and found a willing partner.

He was a young man, supremely confident at sparring with a woman. He spoke to Naomi through his mouth guard as they climbed in the ring. "You ever fought before?"

"Yes," Naomi said, tucking in her own mouth guard with a gloved fist. "You better cross yourself."

He thought it was a joke.

"Where did you learn to fight like that?" the woman trainer asked, after a wrung-out but satisfied Naomi climbed through the ropes several rounds later. Two hectic patches had appeared on her cheeks, but otherwise she was mostly untouched. Her eyes were clear.

"A retired fighter down in Mexico," she answered as the trainer slipped off her gloves. "He specializes in dirty fighting."

"I can tell. You wouldn't last two minutes in front of the judges in this state. Poor Mikal there is going to piss blood for a week from those kidney punches."

"He could have said stop," Naomi said, feeling chagrined.

"Men." The woman grinned. Her grin faded. "You looked like you were holding back, too."

"I was." Naomi saw images of crushed bones, smashed fingers, gouged eyes.

The trainer turned to two teenage boys behind her. "Roberto and Jason, get in the ring." The slender boys slid through the ropes, smacking playfully at each other. "No horseplay," she chided.

Naomi unwrapped her hands, checked all her fingers. The cotton wraps were well-worn and stained with blood. At least it wasn't her blood. That was the rule, she thought, watching the boys lark around the ring, looking more like best friends than opponents. Mikal came and joined her, holding a cold wet towel to his bruised face. "Can you teach me some of those moves?" he asked her under his breath, during a break in the action. "Maybe another time," Naomi answered.

One of the boys split the lip of his friend, and the two instantly stopped sparring, the hurt one leaning through the ropes. Naomi watched as the trainer reached into her fanny pack and pulled out a piece of cold metal, pressing it tight against the cut. Holding the boy's head with firm hands, she pinched the wound shut, hard. He closed his eyes.

"I'm looking for a man," Naomi began, and told her about the scar-faced man. Naomi described him in detail.

The trainer got a faraway look in her eyes. "Except for the blue jacket, that sounds a lot like Ray, our custodian. He's not much of a custodian, actually. He pushes a broom here for free membership. He's punchy." She said this as if in apology, like it was her fault.

"What kind of punchy?" Naomi asked. She knew that there were brain-damaged boxers who were docile while others were violent, even criminally insane.

"Uhhh . . ." The trainer seemed disinclined to answer.

"Where can I find this Ray fellow?" Naomi asked, her heart beating stealthily.

"You're not going to do him like you just did poor Mikal, are you?" The woman had a glint of mischief in her eyes, but also concern. The hurt boy lowered his head towards his coach, his skin stretched white where her fingers were holding the wound shut. A trickle of blood was on her thumb.

"Only if he deserves it," Naomi said, almost idly. She was watching the boy, the wound, the woman. "If I had wanted to take Mikal down, I would have hit him in the body more," she added, and caught the trainer's knowing glance.

"Ray comes in early Monday mornings. So you've got a few days. And no, I don't know where he lives. It could be behind a dumpster, for how he smells some mornings. If you're looking for scars, he's your man."

The woman slowly removed her fingers. The wound had closed. "We do a lot now to prevent that kind of scarring, but you know— skin tears."

"I know," Naomi said, collecting her bag. "Hearts do, too."

Back at Diane's she found Jerome, his head bowed over *Oregon Revised Statutes: Criminal Procedure, Crimes*. He was sitting at the kitchen table, a plate next to him with hard pretzels, bread and butter pickles, mustards, and slices of sharp cheddar cheese. Naomi ate a piece of the cheese, looked over his shoulder. "Studying for your license?" she asked.

He looked up, saw her rosy cheeks, sweat-dampened hair.

"Work out?" he asked, closing the book.

"I found the boxing gym," she said.

Jerome's dark eyes caught her, warmed her. Usually after fighting, the first thing Naomi wanted was to go to bed. Love and war. Once Jerome had teased her about this, but it had not gone over well. So he stayed quiet. Their lovemaking was something neither of them discussed. He knew that for Naomi it was a sacred thing, but scary. Jerome had been her only lover outside of whatever had happened in her youth, and that was not love. What had happened to her as a child wasn't even sex, he thought. It was grotesque and something he kept far from his mind. Making love to Naomi, he found it easy to forget what had happened to her, because in that moment she was purely herself, smiling, loving him. He had never known anyone else like her and knew he never would. She was his heart.

But their love was like a deep trench, and the vulnerability of it always threatened to pull Naomi down. So she danced with him, close and then far. He was trying to accept this. There might never be a magic moment with Naomi, a time when he could relax and feel all was well. She might always be like this, looking over his shoulder, her eyes cautious.

"I beat up this guy. I feel kinda bad about it."

"He could have said stop."

"That's what I said!"

She took another chair, grinned at him. He grinned back, and they both laughed. It wasn't all better, but it sure was closer than before. "You hungry?" he asked, thinking of the bed upstairs, pushing the plate of pretzels closer to her.

"Actually, I am," she said.

Celia was sitting outside Sisters of Mercy, scratching the bloody bandage around her leg. She had rolled up her jeans so anyone walking by could see the bandage, the blood. She knew what she was doing. She was trying to get attention. See, she wanted to say, I am hurt. Someone care.

But no one did. They walked on by, not even looking at her.

Except for Naomi. She came down the sidewalk, arms swinging, face like a lamp. It was big news on the streets, how the FBI was pulling bodies out of the river down at the old docks. Some of the street people had gone down to watch, but not Celia. She guessed next to dead bodies her spider bite wasn't much news.

Naomi had worry on her brow, but it wasn't the expression Celia knew would be there if any of the girls dragged out of the river were old enough to be her sister. That some would turn out to be girls Celia knew probably didn't even occur to Naomi.

"You're hurt!" Naomi said, crouching near Celia. She reached out, and Celia made a show of pulling away until she saw Naomi's hands. Naomi's hands were rough. She had scars on her knuckles—fights, somewhere along the way—and the nails were clipped short. They were hands that had known life, and this comforted Celia. She let Naomi touch her.

"I'm always hurt," Celia said, hearing how foolish that made her sound.

"Did you get cut?" Naomi asked.

"Spider bite."

"That's not good. That can get infected."

Naomi quickly and professionally unrolled the bandage, peeking at the wound. The edges were raised, the hole angry and red. Celia could smell Naomi's hair, leaning over, and the smell was like apples. Celia closed her eyes, drank in the smell. It made her think of Alyssa. Washing Alyssa's hair with the shampoo from the dollar store, soaping it slowly, rinsing her clean with the old yogurt container at the side of the tub.

"I went to the free clinic," Celia told her.

Naomi stopped. The concern went out of her face. She stopped paying attention to the bite, or to Celia. "I should go there," she said. "I didn't even think of that! The doctor might know something. I'll put up a flyer, talk to them."

Her hand had left Celia's leg. Her face was empty, and it gave Celia one of her shivers. Celia could see that Naomi was thinking about her sister, but there was nothing there to remember. Naomi was missing a ghost.

"I saved the dead spider, here, on my pants," Celia said, quickly, trying to recapture Naomi's attention. She began unfolding the dirty cuff to show her.

But Naomi was rising. "You should keep that bandage clean," she said, as if Celia were another adult. "Who is the doctor up there?"

"I think it's Lopez," Celia replied, turning away. Shutting off.

Celia was puzzled. If Naomi cared so much about children, why did she keep walking by?

Celia watched Naomi walk away. Naomi didn't know it, but she was covered with butterflies. They swarmed all over her, attaching to her new clothes, making them as old as time. She would carry them inside the free clinic, and the tall skinny doctor who looked like Stoner, all grown up with a belly, would not see them either. But they would be there, waiting to comfort her when Naomi heard the doctor say he knew nothing, nothing, nothing.

That was the thing about the butterflies. They could be kind when Celia felt bitter. They could encompass all the beauty of this world even when the skies smarted gray and the old men pulled up at the curb, their dicks already in their hands. Celia closed her mind against the men and went to find the other kids. See ya, Celia, the butterflies said. Celia lifted her small hand and waved good-bye.

Stoner had found a piece of cardboard and written *Homeless please help* on it with a black marker pen he borrowed from the woman who ran Aspire. Stoner had wanted to get a red pen and make it look like he had written in blood. "That'll get them," he had said, but Rich and Celia told him that was stupid; it would just scare the day people.

That had started a truth-telling session where all the street kids started talking about chicken hawks and creeps who had invited them home, and all the weird shit they wanted—the girl with the phone talked about a guy who insisted she fuck him up the ass with his electric toothbrush. That got everyone laughing so hard they fell off the sidewalk. Celia laughed until her stomach hurt. Stoner held up one finger and made a *buzz-buzz* sound, and that cracked them up all over again.

Then Celia saw Naomi walking back along the other side of the street. She looked sad.

Celia must have been staring at her because Stoner said something. "Got the hots for her?" Stoner asked, teasing.

"No." Celia glowered at him.

"Celia's got the hots for the church lady."

"She's not a church lady."

"Oh—what is she then?"

Celia looked at the pavement while the other kids laughed. Rich looked at her, concerned. But Stoner frowned. "Hey, you're not thinking she's *the one*, are you?"

Celia stared down, blushing furiously. She could feel the blood pouring to her cheeks. Rich looked on the verge of saying something, but then pulled back.

"Come on, Celia, you know better than that," Stoner said. "No one down here is going to be your *mommy*."

"I—" Celia didn't know what to say. She looked helplessly at her feet.

"Just don't even think it," Stoner emphasized.

"You're not, are you?" asked the girl with the phone. "I've been on the streets a long time, since I was ten. No one is coming to save you. You better get rid of that shitty thinking fast."

"That's enough," Rich interrupted. "She got the point."

"I hope so!" the girl said. She gave Celia a kinder look. "You're only twelve, right? You got time. Make a plan, like me."

"What's your plan?" Celia's voice was muted.

"I'm going to survive until I'm sixteen. Then I'm going to hitch to Alaska and work the canneries there. You can get a work permit at sixteen. I got it all figured out." She spoke with authority.

"If you're so smart, help me with this sign," Stoner said, and the conversation resumed. Celia snuck a glance up the street. Naomi was gone.

Naomi was driving to the state mental hospital. Jerome was at home, studying for his license test. Naomi liked the idea of each of them doing their own thing. Maybe the last year had brought a little too much togetherness.

The radio was playing the top news story of the day: the FBI had retrieved the bodies of four girls from the dock area. Special Agent Richardson, the man on public radio said, was being close-mouthed about details, but a reporter had heard the girls were all prostitutes. The newscaster said this like it was a relief.

Naomi reached for the dial, turned it off.

The old Datsun was without air-conditioning, but she liked the wind rolling in the window, blowing her hair. Once, Jerome had asked why she never wore her hair up. Reflecting, Naomi had realized that she liked her hair being down because it felt like she was moving even when she was standing still.

The bucket seats were comfy, and the car smelled of long trips. For many years it had been her house on wheels. For almost ten years, in fact. She had kept everything she needed in the trunk, moving from case to case, never staying in one place for long. She had become an expert at finding cheap hotels, eating on the road, and doing her laundry at massive truck stops that always seemed to be playing Steely Dan.

Ahead of her, a turn off the freeway. What was once a horrendous big pink building was now a sweet calm gray, and the rest of the new mental hospital unfolded across manicured lawns and pleasant open walking areas. It was still a prison, and there were still barbed curls of razor wire on the fences and armed guards inside. But the state mental hospital was vastly improved since the days it had inspired movies like *One Flew Over the Cuckoo's Nest*.

She parked in a lot where families left cars, the newer visitors carrying cards, the more experienced with bags of change for the vending machines.

The prune-voiced lead psychiatrist was talking to Naomi. "Oregon statute allows the commitment of anyone posing a threat," he intoned. I know that, Naomi thought with annoyance, trotting after him, but she didn't say anything. She wanted his cooperation. They passed the visiting room, and Naomi dodged tables to follow his rapid, frenetic pace. The families were entering, saying hellos to the men and women at the tables.

She followed his back into their main office, thankfully cooled by a fan. The psychiatrist had a receding high hairline, a rind of colorless hair, a humorless mouth. Astonishing in all this were some of the most caring eyes she had ever seen. The eyes changed his face, made it mobile, human. "Most of our patients were convicted of crimes," he said. "But most of those are minor offenses, like public urination or disturbing the peace. It's a shame they have to get arrested to get treatment."

Naomi sat down heavily in the chair across from his desk. She felt her anxiety run out of her. "I'm looking for my sister," she began, and went on to explain the little she knew.

To her deep surprise, in a few minutes he frowned and said, "She might be here."

Later it was like a dream in slow motion. Naomi had walked into a dayroom to find a young woman looking bewildered at being abruptly summoned from her room. She wore the blue smock and pants of the patients, her yellowish hair cut to her shoulders. Her clean skin spoke of decent living, but her eyes were dull. They fixated on Naomi with a question in them, and the question was one for a stranger.

Naomi found the back of a chair with her hand. "We call her Deirdre," the psychiatrist had said, "because it means 'the sorrowful one.'"

She was in her twenties and fit all the descriptors. Deirdre had been found wandering around a lake in the mountains not far from where Naomi had been found. She had twigs in her hair, a fearful expression on her face, and her mouth was stained with blackberries. From the softness of her body, investigators believed she had been fed, and kept. But where she had come from, no one could figure.

Initially they assumed Deirdre was suffering from selective mutism, the result of severe trauma. It was only after a series of neurological exams that they realized that Deirdre had brain damage. At some point Deirdre had almost died from drowning. Her body worked. Her mind did not. She remembered people and had mastered rudimentary sign language. But she could not say where she had been.

Interviews of everyone who lived near the lake had found no one willing to take responsibility for the young woman, and eventually the police decided she had been dumped. She could have been driven from anywhere. A civil commitment judge had sent her to the state hospital. Her favorite thing to do was play with the cards others used for games. Her favorite thing to drink was chocolate milk.

Naomi held on to the chair as her legs buckled, and looked into the wide face. Are you my sister? she wanted to ask.

The psychiatrist watched, consumed with a professional interest. Once he had helped twins reunite after being separated their entire lives. The men had known it instantly, crying and hugging. Nothing like this encounter.

"Deirdre, this woman thinks she might be your sister," the doctor said, making the sign for sister off his chin.

Deirdre looked at Naomi and frowned.

"Is there anything you want to ask her?" the psychiatrist asked Naomi.

"I want to know if she remembers . . . being underground," Naomi said, taking a deep breath. Her cheeks pinked. Her eyes teared up, looking at the floor. "I want to know if she remembers me singing about the sweet chariot."

A hand touched her. It was soft and impersonal. Deirdre was looking right at her, into her. No, she shook her head.

"Thank you," Naomi whispered, her voice strangled. The psychiatrist smiled at Deirdre. He looked at Naomi with sympathy. "I'm sorry for all you went through," he said. "The both of you—wherever she is, too."

Naomi left, running for her car. She saved the tears for the drive home.

* * *

Once, when Naomi was in community college, studying criminal law, a woman who had survived a terrible flood came to talk. She talked about the waters coming over their lands when she was a child, and how she climbed to the roof of their barn, hoping to survive. Days later, rescue workers found her blistered with sun. The waters had receded, revealing the tops of the trees in their yard, and tangled in the branches of those trees were large pillows.

Only they weren't pillows. She realized years later those were her parents.

The other students had questioned the woman, the fear obvious on their own faces. What if we are all capable of lying to ourselves? But the story didn't bother Naomi. Instead it reassured her, confirming that the stories we tell ourselves have more meaning than the facts. That doesn't make them lies. Seeded with every myth was the emotional truth.

Can you come home?"

It was Alyssa whispering over a nighttime phone. Celia stood straight, felt the fear rush right up her back to the sky.

She was on the row with the others, watching the cars circle like so many metal vultures. The girl with the phone had brought it to her. Celia, breathless with anxiety, thought it was her mom, calling the last number back. "Yeah?"

But it was Alyssa, of the soft little voice. She was sobbing, quietly, that swallowed kind of crying that Celia knew too well, that broken-voiced whisper that reminded her of bed slats and the cry of the wind late at night.

"Please come."

Teddy was in the background, yelling for her to give over the fucking phone. Celia could remember the sounds of Teddy's rage carrying out the open windows. She remembered the slammed windows of other houses, the waiting for the dialing for help, the police cars and the heavy knock on the door. Her mother, wiping her cheeks with her hands, giving fearful glances to Teddy, and Teddy opening the door to the police with a regretful smile on his face. All was well here, sir. Never mind the girl hiding in the corner, and the woman sitting on the couch, scratching her arms to ragged sores with desperation and fear.

"Did he hurt you?" Celia asked, and this was the thousand-dollar question.

"Yes—I," her sister answered, and Celia closed her eyes. She saw herself bounding there on huge dragon feet, smashing the house with her claw hand and reaching in to rescue her sister.

"I have to take the bus," she promised Alyssa. "I'll be there."

It was midnight when the last bus finally crawled down their street, and Celia got off, knowing she was stuck out here for the night. She ran up the street, seeing how dark the house was now, the hulking shape of Teddy's truck parked outside, the teamster sticker in the back window. The wind moved through the long grass of the yard, and from inside she heard . . . nothing. A tick of silence. Far away an owl called.

Creeping through the long grass, Celia slid up alongside her sister's bedroom window. It was the bedroom that once belonged to Celia. The same bed, even, filled with sickness. Sometimes Celia thought the mattress was forever wet with the pollution he left. Teddy.

She scratched at the window. Nothing. Pulling her hands along the aluminum seams, Celia felt for the metal runners. She was an expert now at popping cheap windows out of their metal frames.

Her sister unlatched the window, slid it open a bare inch.

"Celia?" It was a whisper, and relieved, Celia collapsed against the side of the house.

"Alyssa? You okay?" she breathed.

"I'm okay." The whisper was calmer now. "You should leave."

"I came all this way."

"I know." Both of them breathed in the night. Celia could smell the inside of the room through the open window, and her nose prickled at the aroma. No.

"He's doing it to you," she said, her heart breaking inside.

A sniffle, and a wipe of the nose. "You should go. He's going to hear you."

"Where's Mom?"

"You know." The image of a couch hung between them.

"You don't have to stay."

"Where would I go?" Her sister's voice was so young. "The teachers say I'm smart. I don't want to live on the streets. Like you."

I was smart, too, Celia thought. But not smart enough. The familiar smell coming from inside the room was stronger now, and Celia's heart dissolved in pain. The smell of sadness and fear and what a man did because of all that. The juice of hate.

"You can tell someone," she whispered, closing her eyes, knowing that was crazy; no one would believe Alyssa, especially now. They would say Celia had talked her into it. She reached out, stroked the rough siding like it was her sister, there on the other side of the—

A sound in the grass behind her and suddenly he was *there*, taller than the night and angrier than the sky, his head above her, and he was swinging at her as she howled in pain. "Caught you, you bitch!" Teddy yelled, and Celia burst into tears as Alyssa did, too, in sympathy. Celia was being shaken by her stepdad, smelling his angry fish breath, seeing how much he wanted to bite her—it was one of her biggest fears, being bitten, and she remembered afresh how he would play those ugly teeth against her childhood nipples and threaten to do just that. "You'd like that, you'd like that," he would say—

He swung her hard against the side of the house. The air escaped her lungs when her head cracked against the wood. She fell to her knees into the grass, dimly aware that the spider bite on her leg was bleeding.

A neighbor's back porch light flashed on. "Don't make me call the cops on you, fucking creep!" someone yelled, and Teddy's arm stopped above her, raised like a sword.

Instead he flipped her over, falling down on his knees, too, and Celia felt him, hard against her like a dog. No, not right here, she thought, and felt that long arm reach around and pin her stomach against her spine so she couldn't breathe. His voice was coarse in her ear. "You'd like that, wouldn't you, ugly little bitch."

Celia tried to breathe. He wouldn't. He would. His other hand came around, to grab her throat, and all of the horror of the world stole over her. The sky was turning black. He was whispering, talking to her, telling her all sorts of secrets. On the other side of the wall Alyssa was sobbing, and Celia was making her promise in her mind to not listen. Go someplace else, Alyssa, she thought. Think of the butterflies.

He stopped. Other lights were turning on. Celia came to, slowly, hearing the tap of his breath, becoming aware of her own limbs.

She wasn't dead after all. She wormed out of his hold and stood up, feeling his grossness all over her body, imprinted through her clothes. He stood, too, looking strangely shamed in the night. On the other side of the wall Celia could hear Alyssa sobbing. She was pleading, under her breath, saying, "Don't hurt my sister, I will do anything."

Celia breathed into the night. Her throat burned. She felt herself coming back, heard the murmur of voices, the secrets he had told. Suddenly she knew. Bending over, swept with nausea, she spoke:

"I wasn't the first," she said. "You hurt other girls. You made my mom an addict, just so you could have me. It wasn't the first time either, you fucking disease."

"You don't know shit, Celia." He wiped his mouth.

"I do know! You raped me! Now you're raping my sister! *You are a fucking rapist.*" The last came as a shout, and around the neighborhood a silence fell. All the murderous rage of Celia's life was coming out now, she was boiling and she didn't care, she was going to run, run, from this horrible man and this terrible life.

"I am not a liar," Celia screamed into the night.

TWO

—

CHRYSALIS

It was early Monday morning, and that meant Naomi arrived at the boxing gym before it opened. She snuck up to the broad glass to make sure it was empty, and then retreated to her car to watch for the mysterious Ray. If he was the same scar-faced man she had seen downtown, she wanted to keep her distance. To start.

She drank the coffee resting in her console, ate a granola bar without tasting it.

Ten minutes before the place was due to open, a group of teenagers showed up and sat politely outside on a piece of concrete barrier. One rose, looked in the dark window, gestured down the street at a Jack in the Box. The others rose to follow him.

A hulking figure walked across the street, towards the gym. From the angle Naomi couldn't see his face. He wore a baseball cap, pulled tight over his temples, and had his collar turned up. His walk was sloping, almost jerking. Nerve damage, Naomi thought. She put down the granola bar, reached for the door handle.

The man walked to the gym door, pulled out a mess of keys,

tried to find the right one with his shaking hand, finally unlocked the door.

Naomi slipped from her car, softly closed the door, and moved swiftly across the street. In moments she was behind him, following his back as he entered the gym, the door still open. Her leather shoes made no sound.

The door shut behind them.

The door jangled.

Ray turned.

He was an older man with a small face, perched like a dried apple on his oversized neck. The small mouth had a strange beauty: pummeled so much it had taken on the appearance of a purpled fig, radiating lines to his still mercifully full cheeks. His friendly eyes were so cut with scars, they looked like he'd had a date with a hedge trimmer. And under his hat, perched like two little Brussels sprouts, were a pair of cauliflower ears. His face reminded her of the hors d'oeuvres that Mrs. Cottle had made for church socials, with vegetable crudités stuck with toothpicks on a cabbage, the inside hollowed out for dip. Mrs. Cottle called these "horse dubbers."

He took a step back, startled. Naomi raised her own hands with caution, turning them to show her palms.

"I don't have no money, miss," Ray said.

"It's okay," she said. "Mistaken identity. I'm sorry to startle you."

"You come to box?"

"No." Naomi shook her head, and then reconsidered. As long as she was here. Her bag was in the back of her car.

"Thank you for coming in," Mike Morton told a still sweaty Naomi, who had rushed to the morgue after his call. She was aware she needed a shower. She pressed her armpits closed.

Mike reached for a model plane and held it in his hands. "I followed your advice and paid a visit down in the capital." Naomi waited, looking at him across his desk, his gray skin a silver color next to his scrubs. She didn't think that was why he had called her. She assumed he wanted her to look at the new bodies they had found.

"I found a researcher. She ran what we know about all the girls we've found—age, physical specs—through their databases. You were right. Some of the girls had been in foster care before they were on the streets. She's confirming their identities right now."

Naomi smiled. It was a vestige of her usual smile, but she was glad to help.

Mike took a deep breath, steadied himself. "There's more. When I was down there, I was looking at these old photos of the state orphanage outside Elk Crossing, on their office walls."

Naomi felt a sense of foreboding.

"There was this photo with a line of girls outside, dressed in winter parkas. There was snow on the ground. In the middle of the group stood a little girl who looked a lot like you. She was maybe three or four and holding the hand of her baby sister. I asked the researcher about it. She told me a story how over twenty years ago, two sisters went missing from that orphanage."

"Who do I talk to?" Naomi barely managed to find the words.

He pushed a number at her. "This is the woman who used to run the orphanage."

▸

RENE DENFELD

Once called Claremont, then Fairfield, the state girls' home was a place of sour ghosts. You could feel it, stepping inside. Like in all institutions, only bad things had happened here.

Naomi had driven a few hours to get there, noting as she passed the small towns along the freeway how she was retracing a path back to her captivity. The orphanage wasn't far from the woods where she and her sister had been held underground. She passed thick forests that would have seemed beautiful to others but sent a shiver of fear through her. Something about the tangled underbrush, the manzanita and sword fern among the chaos of the trees, said *here* to her. And in the woods of her imagination she ran and ran.

Naomi stood in the decayed main hall and tried to remember. Did she hear the sound of running feet, the hushed whispers of little girls? The wet sweep of a mop, the taste of corned beef and cabbage? She could feel the memories in the background of her mind.

"I'm pleased you could come." The retired woman held out spring-cold hands. Naomi could see rims of dirt in her broad nails; she liked gardening. She stared deeply into Naomi's eyes. "I didn't think it could be true . . . You *are* her. The older Bolen sister."

Naomi closed her eyes. She now had a last name. She was someone, not just a nameless girl born from the dirt. A shiver began in her feet and moved up through her legs, making her feel faint. Bolen. My name is Bolen.

"Are you all right?"

"Yes." Naomi's eyes were closed.

She now had a past. A mother. This woman was going to tell

her about herself. The long-sought past was rushing up to her, a voice crashing through the woods behind her. It might pull her all the way back down the trapdoor, down the metal rungs she now felt with her hands. Into a room where she had whisper-sung to her little sister.

But she had to.

"I'm sorry. It must be hard."

"Life is always hard," Naomi said, her own voice tough. She opened her eyes, brought back the smile. "Tell me about myself."

They walked the grounds, the beds of soil loamy and turned over for spring. A set of gardeners were at work, shoveling compost. Inside, down cavernous halls where girls once lined up for dinner, were various parts of machines, broken down. The dining hall was empty, only the shadows of the tables on the floor. A desolate industrial-sized kitchen in the back where men were tearing the wiring out from the walls.

"You came just in time," the silver-haired woman said. "The building sold a few months ago. They're making a lodge out of it, one of those fancy hotels." She gave a skeptical laugh. "Lord knows the nightmares the guests will have, the ghosts that haunt this place."

Upstairs, climbing stairwells worn by hundreds of small feet, they reached a narrow hall, with bedrooms off each side. Without thinking, Naomi marched directly down the hall and turned into a bedroom. Peeling wallpaper covered the walls—dogs and puppies. Naomi looked at the wallpaper, then out the window, to where the gardeners were working below. To the east, not far at all, was the town of Elk Crossing and the woods. She hadn't thought to come here because there had been no reports that even mentioned the orphanage.

"You knew this was your room," the woman said behind her, in wonder. "You and your sister. We tried to keep siblings together. It's never good to keep children in orphanages, but . . . we did our best."

"Do you remember me?"

"Yes."

Naomi felt the pulse in her neck. She had come without Jerome yet again. But she had told him why. She needed to be alone for this, her genesis. This was where it had started.

"We had a hundred and sixty girls living here, and dozens of staff working. Some of the staff stayed nights. I was one of the ones who came and went, from my house nearby."

Naomi wondered why the woman was telling her all this. Guilt, probably.

"Staff—we called them counselors—did head counts every morning. One morning they did a head count, and two girls were missing from this room. Naomi and Sarah Bolen."

Sarah, Naomi marveled.

"At first we thought maybe you had escaped, to run back home. But I knew that wasn't likely."

"Why not?" Naomi asked, but part of her knew.

"You were orphans. Your mother died giving birth to Sarah. That's why you came into care. You had no surviving relatives. You were all alone in the world."

"Except for each other," Naomi said in a husky voice. She lifted the back of a hand and wiped her eyes. "Did you check all the staff?"

"You're smart. I'm not surprised you went into this line of work."

Naomi waited.

The woman sighed. "All accounted for. There were no clues, no leads. It was as if both of you had just vanished in the night."

"What happened then?" Naomi's voice was low.

"Nothing."

The two women squared off in the room, with its decaying wallpaper, the marks where the teeth of multiple beds had dug into the floor. "We called the courthouse in Elk Crossing, but nothing seemed to happen." Naomi frowned. She didn't recall seeing any reports of missing sisters from that town. "Eventually everyone moved on. Of course we didn't forget. I never forgot. But everyone else did. Life just moved on. I moved on. I am sorry."

"I need my records." Naomi swallowed.

An hour later Naomi left, tires crunching down the long drive. A slim file lay in her passenger seat. She silently talked to it as she drove. Sarah. Now I know your name, too. Sarah Bolen. We are sisters. I was barely four and you were only two when we were taken. That's why I can't remember anything before captivity.

And I don't want to remember what happened during it.

The file said more: Names of her mother and her father, who had died in a factory fire not long before Sarah's birth. Relatives, all deceased. Hometown. Birth dates. Naomi now had a birthday—until now she simply celebrated it in the spring, the time of birth. "My forever child," Mrs. Cottle had called her, encouraging her to see every day as her awakening to life. Blood types, medical histories. Each word was a clue, a treasure.

From this Naomi could find her own story. Their mother and father were dead, but she had a past. A lineage. Someplace out there, there would be other Bolens, and she could find them and say, I know you. You are family.

But first she had to find Sarah. And the way to do that was to find the man who had stolen them both.

Driving back, all she could think was, Jerome. I need you, she thought. I hope you are there.

It took most of a night and a morning for Celia to get downtown because she didn't have any bus fare and had to walk all the way. By the time she finally got back—to a big hug from Stoner and Rich—her feet and legs hurt. At least the spider bite had stopped bleeding.

She sat outside the Aspire shelter with a few other kids. Rich had taken off as he sometimes did. Celia thought he had probably gone home, like she did, to check on people who didn't want him. A reporter had come by, asking the street kids if they knew who was killing the girls. "If we knew, wouldn't we tell someone?" the kids asked.

Celia was outside the shelter because of the popsicles. Every week the popsicle man showed up. He was a skinny old hippie who reeked of pot and body odor, and he brought downtown a big cardboard box filled with half-melted popsicles. Over time the kids had figured out the popsicle man was okay. No one had died from eating one of his popsicles, and to their knowledge he had never skeeved on any of them either. Of course no one was letting his dirty fingers anywhere near them anyhow.

He came now, and the street kids gave a little ironic cheer. They gathered round and he opened his box, handing out the purple, red, orange, and green, Celia's favorite. The heavyset woman who ran the shelter came to the gated door, wearing her blue Aspire shirt. She watched them, sympathy in her face.

Shaking her head, she hung the sign for the coming night: FULL.

* * *

"I can tell you like lime."

It was Naomi again. Naomi was on skid row so much it was like she was part of the streets, and even Celia, she had to admit, was looking forward to seeing her, even if it was a mistake, as the other kids said.

Celia had finished sucking the popsicle stick so dry barely even a stain of green remained. That remained on her tongue, which she had been showing to the other kids. They had been sticking their tongues out at one another, making rainbows of purple, red, orange, and green. Sometimes street life could be fun.

"It's okay," Celia muttered, to the ground.

"I'm still looking for my sister," Naomi said. Then she smiled. "But I'm learning more. I've learned her name is Sarah."

"Have you ever had a shower?" Celia asked, suddenly.

Naomi looked puzzled. "Yes."

"Once, when I was little, we went to stay in this scummy hotel. It was because our landlord kicked us out of our house for not paying the rent. The hotel was for poor people—they call it section eight."

Naomi, listening, nodded. She understood.

"I never had a shower before. I didn't understand the curtain goes on the inside. I left it outside."

"Did the water flood?"

Celia's chin trembled. "It poured all over the floor."

"What happened then, Celia?"

Celia looked away. Her face was blank. Naomi waited a long moment, but the girl never answered. "Maybe," Naomi said softly, "you forgot."

Celia's eyes turned towards her. "I never forget."

Celia had been thinking of that day, the pour of golden water down the shower curtain. She had seen it. Oh yes, she had. She had felt the delicious way the water poured over her body, and she had raised her face to the pelting warm rain of it.

Then she had noticed the way the water streamed down the inside of the curtain. She had knelt, hair pouring, and traced her small fingers down the rivulets. She had seen the way they meandered, like creeks in the woods. Some wandered away, thin and delicate and yet brave for doing so, but even they changed course and came back and joined the strong ones. And then all of them ran together, a race, faster and faster, down the plastic curtain, to make brand-new exciting puddles and lakes on the bathroom floor.

For at least an hour the water had pounded down, until it went from hot to cool to cold, and her shoulders thrashed with it, until she felt she was swimming in the iciest lake or ocean—Celia had never swum, but she could imagine it—and the water turned from golden warm to refreshing cold blue. She was now a waterborne creature, swimming in the deep. She was a new kind of chrysalis, rising from the shore. She was a pupa. She had wings; she was a golden butterfly flying over open water. She was tired. Her wings were wet.

She had suddenly come to and realized the bathroom floor was covered with water. Not just covered. Flooded. Celia was naked, kneeling in the tub, red with cold, and she saw her hand, shaking, reach out to turn off the tap. Drip. Drip. The last of the cold water ran down the drain. But the floor of the bathroom was still covered. Inches of it, sloshing around the rusted coffee can they used for trash. Soaked through the stack of stiff towels on the floor. Ruining the toilet paper left by the cracked porcelain bowl.

Moaning, she had stepped out. She heard shouts of fury from the hotel room below her. The stampede of feet from outside. Teddy, awoken from his nap in front of the television, buried in beer cans.

That was when Celia did stop remembering, so what she had told Naomi was kind of a lie. She did remember, only she chose to forget. But that was a different kind of pretend.

* * *

Rich got off the last bus to a late-night street sparkling with dew. The buildings were slick with moisture, a fog billowing down the streets. The dead hours, he thought, before dawn. When the world might rise again. But only if Mother Nature allowed it.

He was a boy of many thoughts, all carefully hidden. All through school, even before his dad was sent to prison, before his mother turned into the laughingstock of not just their town but the entire world, he had kept his thoughts to himself. He didn't want anyone to laugh at him, too.

The video of his mother still pained him. He wondered if any of the millions who watched it ever thought she was a real person, dancing on that roof, smashing a beer can against her head. Rich remembered the video in colors of red and veins of black, taken by a laughing stranger with a phone camera.

Child Protective Services had come a few days after the video went viral. They had put Rich in the social worker's car. They had left the fetid house, the piles of empty bottles, left his mother. They had punished her for being human, for making the same mistakes others did off camera.

He walked quickly, hurrying through the dark, empty streets. He had waited too long to catch the bus. He figured Celia and Stoner had already gone to the overpass. But to get to the overpass, he had to go through the waterfront park, and that, even more so than most their world, was a dangerous place. It was a place without lights, where wilding packs of jocks roamed at night.

Moving as quietly as he could, Rich crossed into the waterfront park, trying to move under the deepest shadows so he wouldn't be seen.

The last time Rich had seen his mother was the day they took him. No, that wasn't really true. He had seen her once more, at a visit in the child welfare offices. Her drinking had gotten worse, it was clear. He didn't blame her. His dad had been sent to prison for doing nothing—literally, his dad had been arrested for loitering—and his mom had been working two jobs ever since and still couldn't afford their rent. That was how she started. She was so stressed all the time.

His mom had needed a friend. That was what she had needed and never got. Just one good friend, someone who would come to the house and clean up the bottles and encourage her to take a shower and sit with her until she got herself right.

Not the kids who spray-painted *LOSER* on the side of their house. Or the boss who fired his mom after the video went viral. Or the teachers who looked at Rich and then looked away. Or the group home where he was sent.

There was something behind him.

Rich froze. His thighs prickled with fear, and his stomach somersaulted. Slowly he turned around.

They were right down the path, stalking him. He could see them moving under the cherry blossom trees, coming into view. They came out into the path, and he felt his bowels loosen in terror.

High school jocks. They formed a line across the path.

For a terrible moment he didn't know what to do. The skid row was behind him, all the shelter doors locked for the night. The footbridge was ahead of him. He could dash there, but they could follow. There was no place to run.

He turned and began running for the bridge as fast as he could, knowing it wouldn't be fast enough. All the memories of gym classes and sports events, the efforts of his mom to get him to do something besides play video games when she was at work.

"Hey! Catch the—"

He could hear them gaining behind him, their voices mad with joy and the excitement of pursuit. Rich felt his feet pick up, his legs churn in terror. His mouth was open, gulping air that could not reach his lungs, already burning.

"Fucking fag!"

Rich wished he could close his eyes, melt to the ground in sorrow. The footbridge was ahead of him, but he wasn't going to make it. He could hear them right behind him.

He whipped around before they could tackle him. There were six of them, all in new clothes, windbreakers, sneakers that probably cost hundreds of dollars. Their hair was cut short, their faces strangely plastic, honed to sharpness by razors and cruelty.

"What do you want?" he asked, backing up. He immediately wished he hadn't said anything. His voice cracked with fear.

"Whatcha running for?" the leader asked. He was a muscular boy with bright yellow hair, dyed. He had a diamond in one ear. Rich remembered some old bum telling him that once upon a time that meant you were gay, only now it didn't, but that didn't change anything, did it?

"I'm talking to you. You fucking loser."

The leader was puffing up, his arms turning into deadly triangles. His eyes were like dead fish. He reminded Rich of the body they had seen in the river. Maybe the boy had come from the river, too. Maybe they all had. Maybe they were all already dead, and that was why they played this game.

Rich felt the fear widen, encompass him. *Please*, he wanted to tell the world. Don't do this to me. Again.

"Fucking street trash."

The leader was winding up, relishing. A light dancing, athletic. One of the other boys held up his phone, recording. Another video, Rich thought, as the first fist swung. Taking out the trash, as they called it. By the next night it might hit a million views, and everyone would be laughing at him, too.

Rich felt the first blow against the side of his head. It was like the stars, and the moon, yes, exploding into pain, and he could feel himself dropping, trying to catch his hands on the pavement, thinking dimly maybe they wouldn't want to bloody their new shoes by kicking him. But that didn't work either.

This time Naomi asked Jerome to come with her. It was a bit like the past year of travel: increasingly long silences broken by spontaneous laughter and warmth. Jerome recognized his people's home country as they crossed the valley: long-neglected oak savannas, fertile farmland crested with dark fir mountains.

ELK CROSSING, the bullet-punched sign outside of town said, leaning over a ditch frenzied with spring growth. POPULATION: 740.

Naomi felt her body tense driving into the empty town. A spider was in the back of her skull, hissing danger. This was strawberry country. This was terror.

Naomi and Jerome had come through here before, after finding the bunker nearby. But they had come up empty. Now they had a name. They had a story to follow.

The town of Elk Crossing looked abandoned, the shop windows soaped. They drove past the funeral home, low and squat and pink, with dried shrubs outside the walls like freckles, and a boarded-up high school. The fields were still planted. But the family farms had been eaten up by the corporations that now combed the fields. Few people lived here anymore. It was a place managed, not occupied.

The solitary bar was still open. Naomi watched a man with a face like burlap stagger down the street to his truck.

She parked at one of the forgotten meters.

"What are we looking for?" Jerome asked. Their efforts to find anything online about how Naomi and her sister went missing from the orphanage had been fruitless.

"I don't know yet," she answered.

Naomi was surprised to find the small courthouse was still open. Inside the front entry was a solitary clerk. She looked up, lines of surprise in her face.

"I need to see your records," Naomi said, showing her license. Jerome, next to her, stood, wearing his Purple Heart pin on a white shirt with the sleeve neatly pinned up over the cap of scar tissue from his missing arm. That's all it took. Glancing reverentially at Jerome while completely ignoring Naomi, the clerk hustled. "Right this way," she said, leading them down a hallway floor lined with mop streaks. Naomi rolled her eyes. "Hero," she whispered to Jerome.

Naomi looked around as they walked, at the crumbling walls, the circles of water damage on the ceiling. They passed the solitary courtroom, the heavy doors now latched. The bench outside was polished down by generations of bottoms. Above the bench was a painting of an older man labeled with a brass plaque.

The clerk unlocked a door to a long narrow room lined with shelves. In the middle was an oak table. Naomi walked down the row of brown file boxes, checking dates. All the town records were here: police, court, and land.

"Here," she said, pulling down a box for the months that she and her sister had gone missing. She carried it to the table, surprised at how light it was.

The clerk, her face curious, hung in the doorway. Behind her the pure light of farm-valley Oregon poured into the room. "We're okay," Naomi said so the woman would go away. Naomi shut the door behind her.

The box, as it turned out, was almost empty. They found traffic tickets and divorce decrees, a few deeds. No missing child reports. Jerome and Naomi went through box after box and found the same paucity. There was no sign that the kidnapping had ever been reported, let alone investigated. It was as if she and her sister had never existed.

Jerome set down a land deed. "This doesn't make sense," he said, frowning. "There's no such thing as a town without crime." Naomi leaned over, looked at the signature at the bottom. *Judge Thurman*, it said. She looked at the other records. They all had the same name.

Naomi stood below the painting down the hall. THE HONORABLE RALPH THURMAN, the plaque said. The judge had been a heavy-jowled man with crinkled grandfatherly eyes. She checked out the dates below. He had died not long after she went missing.

"The migrants who found me nearby didn't want to come here," Naomi said under her breath. The clerk was hovering nearby, inquisitive. "They drove me all the way to Opal. There was a reason why."

Jerome stood behind her, waiting.

Naomi turned to the clerk. "Where's the local graveyard?"

The Elk Crossing graveyard had the shy, quiet look of all abandoned places. Naomi and Jerome walked the rows of headstones, passing under tall firs. A mossy statue of Mary reached out her consoling hand, a sparrow nest in her pitted palm. Jerome looked over the grassy oak savannas that were once populated by his people, only to be stolen and now neglected.

In the back, crowded against a falling-down stone wall, they found the baby nursery. Baby nurseries, also called baby graveyards, were a Northwest tradition that went back to pioneer times. Naomi didn't know if other places had the same practice of burying children in a separate graveyard, or if it was just an Oregon peculiarity.

The baby nursery was surrounded with a row of overgrown hedges, almost swallowing an arching cast-iron entryway. Inside was a maze of tiny headstones sunken into the grassy soil. The dates went back to the 1800s. Many, she could tell, were stillbirths. Naomi stopped to read one. *Baby Agnes, Nov. 2, 1901, born already with our Lord.*

Other graves were of children well into their teens. You could almost track epidemics and flus, Naomi thought, walking past the clusters of graves. "This is sad," Jerome said, pointing to a row of five children, all from the same family. Their names told the story, starting with Hope and moving on to Faith and finally the last one, Perseverance. "I wonder if they kept trying," he said.

Naomi didn't respond. She told herself she was used to death, used to being buried alive.

The sun, passing through the trees, caught on Jerome's black hair.

"What do the Kalapuya believe about death, again?" Naomi asked, curious.

Jerome knelt and swept dirt off an ancient headstone with his one hand. "My people believe that no one really dies. When it is time for us to leave this world, one of our loved ones comes to walk us on. They take us to the other country."

"Where is this other country?"

"No one knows. You have to die to find out."

"Well, no thanks."

He rose, brushing dirt off his jeans. "Remember how we used to hunt for their belongings in the trees, Naomi?"

"I do." It sounded like a promise. Naomi gazed in adoration at Jerome.

Her shoe had hit a line of newer graves. This section of the child graveyard was crowded, and Naomi instantly recognized another graveyard tradition: the pauper graves. She was looking down at a cheap metal plate from decades past. She followed down a line of graves. There were over a dozen of them, ending around the time she had gone missing. Each contained a child with an estimated age of five to ten.

Jerome stood next to her. The wind sloughed through the trees. Each of the plates said the same thing: *Child Doe*.

"Something terrible happened here," Naomi said.

"Stop here."

Unaccustomed to Jerome speaking so abruptly, Naomi pulled over. They had just left the town and were passing by another set of strawberry fields. The green crowns were just now budding with white flowers. An old farmhouse stood on a hill, as empty as the sky. A torn scrap of fabric flew out a dormer window. In the pasture was a single majestic white oak tree, its tightly budded arms reaching for the sky.

Jerome got out. Naomi followed.

Finding the rusted pasture gate, Jerome walked into the field. The unruly grass came to his waist. The air was heavy with the rich scent of cottonwoods, the fences draped with the long white blooms. Jerome walked until he came to the spreading, majestic oak.

He stood underneath the tree and lifted his one hand and squinted. Naomi, curious, looked up, too.

Tied high up in one of the branches was what appeared to be an old blanket, wrapped tightly around bulky objects. The bundle was securely tied to the tree with ancient rope. The rope was so old the tree limb had overgrown part of it, swallowing it. The blanket was tufted from birds and rotten in places, dried hard by the sun in others.

"Well, after all this time, I think we found one of the relics we were looking for as kids," Jerome said, smiling at Naomi.

"Do we climb up there, take it down?" Naomi asked.

Jerome shook his head. "I should get an elder from the tribe. If it is an ancestor's belongings, I don't want to be disrespectful. It's been there for years. It can wait a few days."

In the distance the farmhouse, empty windows for eyes, seemed to smile. The breeze lifted Jerome's hair, and the skin of his arm looked dark under the tree. All around the cottonwoods bloomed, the soft down catching on the wind.

On the way back to the city it began raining.

Heading back downtown from the overpass was miserable when it was raining.

Celia and the boys had waited for what felt like hours hoping the cloudburst would stop, crouched in their overpass cave. The heavy rains soaked under the bushes, running in wet muddy fingers up to their feet.

Finally, too hungry to bear it any longer, they slid down the hill, getting covered in mud, and ran, squelching in sopping-wet shoes, to the freeway, where the cars, wipers on full tilt, didn't even slow down for them. Celia could see the faces of the drivers huddled over the wheels. She wondered if she would ever learn to drive. Her mother had lost her license for driving while high. Celia understood that was punishment, but she didn't think the judge understood that meant her mom couldn't work anymore and that meant Teddy owned them and Celia was trapped forever.

Finally a break in the traffic came, and the street kids ran, their jeans black with water. Rich kept his head down, his swollen lids almost closed with bruises. They crossed the footbridge, the river below them a wild torrent. Celia could see the back of Stoner's neck where the rain had parted his hair, the twin tendons as delicate as musical instruments.

The street kids went to the deli at the top of downtown. The booths were made of a sticky fake leather that made squishing noises when they sat down. The waitress put the water glasses down, stared at Rich and his swollen, bruised face. "Someone beat you up, honey?" she asked with concern.

No, he shook his head, miserable.

"Let me guess," she addressed them. "Biscuits and gravy."

"I want pie. Pecan, à la mode," Stoner said, and a rivulet of water poured down his neck. Celia stared at him. That was a stupid thing to buy. Pie was more expensive and didn't last as long. Biscuits and gravy was big and cheap.

The plates came, heavy and white. On the plate in front of Celia, thick white goo was ladled over two stale biscuits with dry crumbs on the sides. Celia stuck a fork in one, twanged it. She pulled the fork out. Most of the gluey biscuit came with it, tiny pieces of gray mystery meat in the pasty white gravy. She put the chunk on her tongue. It tasted like salt and nothing else. She was hungry. She ate it.

Rich had come back late the night before, crawling into their cave, whimpering. Celia had woken just enough to smell the blood. She had lain against him until he stopped shivering, putting her arms around his cold middle. Waking, she had seen he had been beaten. With the others she had counted his teeth, made him lift his shirt so they could see that his ribs, though bruised, were not broken. His breath had whistled in and out okay, and his eyes, though bloodied, could see. A beating was ordinary and deeply sad. But ordinary. Or so she told herself, once again.

Celia thought about the apartments and trailer courts they had lived in when she was little, with names like Pine Top Estates and Chantilly Arms. The grosser the place, the nicer the name. It almost felt like a personal insult.

Stoner ate his pie in three bites. Then he waited to see if anyone wasn't going to finish their food, his lowered eyes checking, then coming back again.

Rich ate, head down, fork moving rapidly from plate to mouth. You could tell it hurt Rich to eat, but he did it all the same. They all kept their arms cocked around their plates, like someone might steal them.

Celia looked out the window. Sometimes she wanted bad things to happen just to relieve the moments like this. Like the way her feet itched in her wet socks, or the way her soaked jeans clung to her icy thighs, getting colder by the second. The feeling of needing to go to the bathroom.

The food was gone. They pulled out wet pennies and linty nickels, counting their change onto the wet table. Stoner licked his plate. The waitress watched from behind the counter, then went into the kitchen.

In a moment the waitress came back, bearing another white plate. Biscuits and gravy for Stoner. She put down the plate with a smile. "Manners," she reminded him.

"Thank you," he mumbled.

"You looked hungry," she said, looking relieved.

When they left, she waved at them, and Celia turned around, waving back.

There was one good thing about a heavy rain:

It got rid of the creeps. The pimps, the freaks, and the johns.

The only people on skid row when it was raining were the street people and the nuns and the volunteers trying to help. Those people were real. They didn't tell lies like *go to the police if anyone touches you* or *it will all be okay*.

One of the nuns came down the wet sidewalk now as the homeless huddled under the gusts of rain and wind. Families protected their children under their coats. The nun handed out clear white plastic rain ponchos, knowing the street people liked these best—you could see through them to make sure another was not holding a weapon—and they kept the water off better than any jacket.

Grateful, the street people donned the ponchos, and Celia and her friends became one in a line of white plastic gleaming objects. "Like a row of condoms," Stoner joked, his mouth wet with rain, but Celia thought more like pictures she had seen of jellyfish, bobbing along in a gray pavement sea.

In the late afternoon the sky cleared and became a hard metallic blue. The sun shone, and the mist evaporated off all the buildings, twining like snakes off the turrets. It got so hot that the metal trash cans were warm under their touch as Celia and Rich dug into them, looking for returnable bottles others had missed. It was then that Celia noticed the ponchos littering the street. The families had returned to holding their kids in front of their jackets, and it was like everyone had forgotten the rain.

With the heat came danger.

Stoner, living up to his name, got into something wicked. Only instead of smoothing him out, relaxing his always tense face, it turned his mouth into a black cavern full of teeth, and Celia, like the others, ducked and ran from his swinging-wide fists.

"Slow down, Stoner, slow down," Rich kept saying, getting chased in a circle in the hot street, the sun pounding down. The bums, lying on their sides in the heat, panted and watched the show. Stoner spun and spun, and Celia and the other street kids stood under the ASPIRE sign and watched, heads cocked for—

There. The sound of sirens. The cops only came when there were fights. Or bodies on the streets. No one ever knew who called the cops since skid row was all street people. Maybe it was the re-covering alkies sulking in the dirty rooms above, sent there by the agencies to test the dry among their friends.

The cops came to a halt, sirens muted by the day, the sun striking off the domed lights. They got out of the car. One walked towards Stoner, talking to him. Another stood to the side, watching, hand on his gun. Celia was watching, too, her head tilted. She became cautious, times like this. She became an eye in the sky.

Were the cops going to kill Stoner? That was the worry in her mouth, and the cynical fear in the eyes of the bums. But the cop talking to Stoner soon had him cornered, and he had his hands up. Profanity was pouring out of his mouth. "Fucking cocksuckers,"

Celia heard. "Clit fuckers." My friend is high, she wanted to tell the cops.

But the cops seemed to know. They pushed Stoner into the back of the car, cuffed. In a moment they were driving off, Stoner's curly hair visible through the window. The kids could hear him yelling from inside the car.

"Where do you think he's going?" Celia asked Rich after coming down from the clouds. She realized several minutes had passed. Rich had been watching her, curiously.

"Juvie, I bet," Rich said. "Maybe he'll get some help now."

Celia looked at him, sideways. It had never occurred to her that Stoner needed help. Or that any of them might get it.

Celia awoke under the overpass, her mind as smooth as stone. Only the butterflies were there, caressing her awake just as they had carried her to sleep.

She had never told anyone about the butterflies. She knew people would shake their heads, like she was being stupid. Girls like her were damaged, broken, not worthy of the butterflies. Even the victim advocate in court had acted like Celia was slime you could wipe up, but the stain would remain. When the victim advocate had said Celia could move on to a good life, the lie on her mouth never reached her eyes.

But Naomi—she was different. Naomi wasn't afraid of what had happened to Celia. She acted like Celia wasn't broken at all. Which was funny, because when Celia was around Naomi, she didn't feel broken either.

Celia turned over. Rich lay next to her. He opened his eyes, and the two of them just looked at each other, for the longest time.

* * *

In the butterfly museum, Celia knew, nothing dead is allowed. Inside the museum is the soft velvet of plants, the smell of moisture and the lick of leaves. The rooms there hum with spirits, and they are like a movement you can feel but not hear. There is the soft crunching of leaves, the spiraling crawl of the caterpillars, and the soft dusky noises of the instars inside their shells.

In the butterfly museum the butterflies flit from plant to plant, moving their majestic wings in absolute, pure peace. There are no predators there. You can go in, and the butterflies will accept you. You can stand in the middle of the rooms, among all the basking plants, the fruitful air, and you will be one of them. If you hold very still, they will come to you. They will land on your arms, and your head, and, yes, even your cheeks, and they will touch you like you are the most tender piece of fruit or the sweetest pollen of any flower.

You will know then. All their life they have been waiting for you.

I might have found something," Jerome told his friend Ed Ashtree.

Jerome had driven down to see him. It was only a few hours out of the city but a world apart, in the chilly coastal ranges. He had found Ed chopping wood at his house, an unfriendly-looking manufactured home in a gully, damp with stunted trees, festooned with moss. "This is a bad country," Jerome remembered a chief had said of this inhospitable land over a century before, after his people had been forced to march here. "It is cold and sickly. There is no game on the hills and the people are dying."

Ed, sixty-two years old with a seamed face, had befriended Jerome on his first trip to the reservation a few years before. Standing in the tiny library, Jerome had looked lost. Ed, recognizing a fellow Kalapuya from his features, offered greetings.

"What?" Ed asked, yanking the axe out of the stump. The wood was so rotten it split at a touch. The damp got in everything here.

Jerome explained the bundle tied in the tree. "It's in a white oak tree, in what used to be our people's country."

Jerome felt comfortable with Ed, in a way he had never felt before with anyone else. That first day, wandering around the reservation, Jerome had realized he was seeing other natives. It was a feeling he didn't try to explain to Naomi, who was used to looking like she belonged, even if she felt different inside.

"Our people used to burn those fields, to preserve the white oak savannas," Ed said. "We were among the first to practice wildfire control that way. For the acorns, the huckleberries, the deer." A thin spire of wood smoke from the house punctuated his words.

Ed, like Jerome, was one of only a few thousand Kalapuya left, from a mighty nation that once ruled the valleys. After being almost eradicated by epidemics, the few survivors of their people had been forced to this sickly land. A civilization that had flourished since the ending of the Ice Age, almost wiped out in less than a few hundred years.

"Do you want to go check it out with me?" Jerome asked.

Ed gave Jerome a puzzled look. Jerome was so clearly hungry to know his people, and yet he acted as if he didn't matter. Maybe it was growing up in foster care. Jerome had bought into the lie that some histories matter more than others, and this angered and grieved Ed.

Ed thought Jerome played second fiddle to Naomi, even though he was a decorated soldier, a war hero. "Of course I want to check it out," he replied testily, and then softened. "Stay the night here. We'll go back in the morning."

"Naomi will miss me. I'll meet you there."

"Naomi can take care of herself," Ed said, picking up the rotting split wood and adding it to the stack.

Jerome thought of all the times Naomi woke shaking from nightmares and he held her. Since they had started looking for her sister, he often awoke to find Naomi pacing the floor, restlessly, fast asleep but ready to search. "I'll meet you there," he said.

Jerome realized he had the better part of a day—a few hours to sunset—before he needed to head back to the city. The ocean beckoned, over the rest of the scrubby mountains. Manzanita and bent pines, hills that rode back from the winds and trees that remained, stubby reminders of faith and perseverance.

He drove into a tiny, ramshackle fishing town. On a sand dune covered with bladelike sea grass, he stood watching the fishing boats ride the waves directly onto the shore, sparkling with the last of the sun. The cold sand was empty except for one lone woman walking with a tea cozy hat on her ample gray hair and a long coat.

Jerome wondered what he had wanted to find out here besides memories of the long years between Naomi leaving their foster home and them getting married. They were lost years, and not even the scurry into war had helped him feel like he had a cause in this world besides loving her. He kept this hidden from her because he was terrified of how helpless it made him feel. He knew some would say he loved too much, too deeply, but he asked himself what else on the earth were we here for.

He got into his truck and drove back to the only home he knew, which was her.

Naomi was standing outside the Aspire shelter. The smeary brick, the narrow streets, the shapes huddled in the doorways—all felt familiar to her now. She had crossed the threshold. The world of the missing had become her own world. She knew the regulars, the bruised-cherry alcoholics, the families on nodding acquaintance, the street kids like Celia.

And the scar-faced man.

He was at the corner. He turned to see her and their eyes met. Naomi moved towards him, quickly, at a trot, dodging through the street people.

But when she got to the corner, he was gone. She blew her breath out in exasperation.

A small, fussy-looking man in round glasses was standing nearby. He had been studying one of her flyers, taped to a telephone pole. His face was as round as his glasses, with a narrow, upturned nose. He wore a suit, even in the warmth of the day. His neat little bow tie reminded her instantly of Sean Richardson, and she remembered his talk of an undercover agent. This man's shorn silver hair was a dead giveaway he was a cop.

"Do you know who that man is?" Naomi asked him.

"I have been wondering that myself," the man replied in a soft, cultured voice. The sun flashed off his glasses. She noted his shiny black dress shoes. Not even trying to fit in, she thought. She lost even more respect for the Feds.

"Have we met before?" Naomi asked, politely. "Maybe at a training?" She was thinking of all the law enforcement classes she had taken where the FBI showed up, acting dark and aloof in the back rows. He tilted his barbered head at her.

"I'm sure we have," he said.

Naomi was moving up the library stairs, feeling the dense air. The air of a thousand books, hanging serenely over the heads at the tables.

She was on her way to the third floor to look at old microfiche for the town of Elk Crossing. She had a lot to learn. Exactly what she wasn't yet sure. Libraries had been the saving grace of many of her cases. Old phone directories, ancient city maps, blueprints, self-published biographies—you never knew what you might find. She cracked one missing child case because a corner store grocer had written a diatribe against the Piggly Wiggly chain and, unbeknownst to himself, given away the location of his disappeared son.

She was passing the fiction room, and there, perched like an urchin in one of the wood chairs, reading as if all alone in a magical universe, was Celia.

Naomi slid into the chair across from Celia, making sure to cough first. She didn't want to startle the girl. Celia looked up, her expression cold—probably expecting a pervert—and then her face changed with surprise. She looked possibly even happy to see Naomi.

Naomi smiled at the stack of books around the girl, along with scraps of paper. Butterflies and more butterflies and, perhaps to mix things up, a few novels. About butterflies. FLIGHT BEHAVIOR, read the thick spine of one. Barbara Kingsolver. That's a serious book, Naomi was on the verge of saying, but stopped herself. It might sound insulting to the bright girl.

Celia looked over Naomi's head as if she saw something there.

Naomi looked around, saw nothing but the ornate ceiling. The girl had been drawing something, but she hid it with one hand, pulling the paper closer to her.

"I'm doing research about my sister," Naomi said. Her hands were relaxed on the table.

Celia looked interested. "What kind of research?"

"Oh, you'd be surprised at what you can find in the library." Naomi paused and then said, directly, "It's hard to keep secrets. Sooner or later they come out."

Celia looked slightly sick. Her soft hand hid the drawing. "Sometimes people don't believe you even when you do tell," she said.

Naomi could feel the silence around them. She had suspected it, but now knew it to be true. People act as if reporting childhood sexual abuse solved the problem, but Naomi knew that most cases don't end in conviction. What no one talked about was what life was like for the victims after acquittal.

"I did everything right," Celia said.

"I'm sure you did," Naomi answered.

Celia glanced again above Naomi, as if she were seeing something there. Her green eyes were clear and bright. "No one cares," she said. "It's all bullshit."

Naomi felt a twisting. "I care. Same with Jerome, my husband, and lots of others you don't know. There's even an FBI undercover man trying to find out what is happening to the missing girls. People do care, Celia."

"Try to talk yourself into that—huh." Celia picked her book

back up. She held it in front of her so Naomi couldn't see the tears in her eyes. After a while, she heard the chair squeak. She felt rather than saw Naomi leave the room.

Celia looked down at the sketch she had been working on.

Up the steps into the periodicals room. Naomi knew she was wronging Celia but was not sure how. *Oh yes, you do*, her mind said.

She unspooled ancient periodicals into the reader. The long-defunct *Elk Crossing Gazette*. Ads for tomato soup and a short-lived beer garden. She combed the obituaries carefully. Warm eulogy for Mrs. Blankenship, who made a mean mince pie. No one liked to cook strawberries in strawberry country, Naomi knew. They were sick as fermented jam of them.

She came to the week she and her sister had been stolen. The most exciting event reported was a log-rolling contest. You'd think nothing bad had ever happened in the town of Elk Crossing. There were no articles about missing children, or the dead and unidentified Child Does buried in the local graveyard. She read until her eyes grew blurry.

She stopped, like her hand was on a Ouija board. *Locals spruce up state orphanage*, read the caption under the photo. Naomi enlarged it. There were no names, no identities. Just a group of men in the orphanage yard decades before, pitching brush into a trailer. One man had turned towards the camera, a hat shading his eyes. Naomi put her face close to the reader, trying to discern features. They were too far away to make out their faces.

Stopping, rubbing her mouth, Naomi was unaware that her eyes had gathered into a dead-set stare. She got up and found the Census of Agriculture. Most people knew that the census counted humans. They didn't know the government also counted every sheep and cow. Returning to her reader, Naomi was again immersed. Thickets of lines and numbers. Dewberries and goats, cows right down to the weight.

Naomi got to the page showing the number of migrant farm workers hired, which got her thinking. She remembered the migrants wrapping her in an old serape the night she escaped, keeping her by their fire. In the morning they had driven her away from Elk Crossing. They had saved her life.

Her fingers following the numbers, she noticed a dwindling workforce. Fewer migrant workers had been willing to work the Elk Crossing strawberry fields as the years passed. It wasn't wages, Naomi could tell. Other towns reported increasing numbers of laborers. She remembered the children buried in the graveyard. If their parents were undocumented migrants, it would explain why others would be unwilling to work the fields. They had known something was very wrong in the town of Elk Crossing.

She stood up, stretched, was surprised to see the sun was setting. Hours had passed. The main room was empty. Celia could have been sitting outside the door in the hall, back against the wall, her special book in hand, waiting, and Naomi would not have known.

Naomi opened the online card catalog, cross-checking names. Elk Crossing newspapers, check. Elk Crossing courthouse, done.

Elk Crossing and strawberries. Now look at this. An old listing for the Thurman Family Strawberry Farm.

Owned by none other than the judge himself, Ralph Thurman.

The lights flickered above her. It was time to go.

Floors below her, Celia had decided to leave, but her warmth was still in the rooms, haunting Naomi with her longing.

L ook." Rich spoke with fear as ripe as the bruises on his face.

He and Celia were at the edge of an industrial area, looking for cans. It was just the two of them now. Word had filtered back, as it sometimes did on the streets, that Stoner was in lockdown treatment. He liked it there, they had heard. They had food.

Celia had thought about telling Rich about the scary house she had seen some weeks before, with the eyes behind the basement window. But Rich might want to go look, and Celia wanted to stay the hell away from it.

The street was cold and empty. The sky was the color of smoke, with a magenta sun, and Celia marveled at how the dumpsters filled up despite how desolate the streets were. She had just pulled out what looked like a completely uneaten and unfucked-with McDonald's burger when Rich spoke. She opened the bun, checking for broken glass. People did mean shit in life.

She froze. Down the street a group of jocks had gathered, climbing on a dumpster. Larking, their faces said. All the old-fashioned words for the hunt, Celia thought, when it stops being play and starts turning wild.

But this wasn't play, unless Rich and Celia were the prey.

"Are they the same ones?" she asked, putting the burger back in the trash.

Run, the butterflies warned, suddenly. They masked the falling sun with their fury.

Rich slowly backed away. "Let's go," he said.

The jocks turned. The leader had yellow hair.

"*Fuck*," Rich said.

For real, the butterflies added. Run, Celia!

Celia ran. She felt as unreal as the coming night sky. Her thin-soled shoes, hitting the rough road. Her legs, lifting the sun-dried jeans. Her mouth, breathing the dusky, red-tinged air. None of this was real, a voice in her said, and that was why she might end up a junkie strung to the last hope of life, or a phantasm that went in and out of the cars, nothing but a hollow shell that performed as the men wanted. A doll. A toy. Never was here.

The last fury, the butterflies told her, flying in great clouds now, up by the falling sun, was if Celia was to believe her cells had hope. If she was to claim her body was as real as the blood that might jet from her veins, as real as the cars and the roads and everything else that mattered down here, everywhere. If Celia could only think she was alive.

That would be the most radical act, the butterflies said, coating the sun. If only Celia could think she deserved to live.

"They're getting closer." Rich's mouth was a choo-choo train, collecting breath, his cheeks florid. The two darted around corners, running faster, faster. Through a narrow street, closing in towards downtown, the last stretch of vacant road, littered with the empty warehouses that posted security guards so the homeless could not camp. FOR SALE FOR DEVELOPMENT, read the graffitied signs as the two street kids ran, the pack of jocks chasing them, their own faces blurring.

Part of Celia wanted to dart off to the side and run straight at the river, to her own doom. Or to turn around and walk slowly towards them, her arms out, her eyes closed. A sacrifice.

But her body was saying live, and the butterflies were, too, and she and Rich ran.

* * *

"I brought you a book," Naomi said, smiling wide.

Celia was sitting on the curb on skid row, arms wrapped around her legs, deeply ashamed of herself, because in running, she had pissed her pants, and now she didn't know what to do. She could feel the scalding piss on her inner thighs, feel the damp circle in her jeans. If she stood up, the whole world would know.

The butterflies, flitting around, consoled her. They traced her tender skin with their antennae, delighting at her beauty.

Flashes of memory, of all the times she had pissed herself. Sometimes she had pissed on purpose to keep Teddy away, but it never worked. She got spanked instead, and the single wet pair of torn sheets were stripped off the naked mattress, and she had to go back and lie on the cold damp circle. Then there were all the times she had pissed without even knowing it, going home with yet another note in her hand. *Celia smells like piss*, the other kids started saying, which is why Celia never teased Rich for the same. The kids couldn't find a name that rhymed with both *piss* and *Celia*, so they finally settled on calling her "Pee-lia."

Now Naomi was standing above her, pride reeking from every shiny pore, sturdy leather shoes on the filthy pavement, beautiful trouser legs, and holding out in her hand was a brand-new book.

BUTTERFLIES OF THE PACIFIC NORTHWEST, it said.

"It's for you," Naomi added. She sounded like she was all of twelve herself.

Fuck you, Celia wanted to say. She was filled with a sudden rage. I'm sure that book will taste good for *dinner*. Thank you for *nothing*. She turned away. She didn't want to speak because the anger might come out, and she didn't want Naomi to see or hear it. But it was there, settling cold and hard in Celia's chest, rising to her throat, choking her.

"You don't want it?" Naomi's voice, teasing, still light, but now with an edge of concern. The book stayed held out.

Celia shook her head, still looking away, her lips pressed together. Rich, down the row, looked at her. A car horn honked—a john picking up a kid was holding up the line. Naomi turned around, saw the cars, and the realization of exactly what Celia did down here struck her like a cold slap. Moving slowly, she set the book down on the sidewalk, near the girl. "I'll leave it here for you," she said, softly.

Then she walked away, head bowed.

Rich came down the row, sat next to Celia. He took the book.

He leaned over quick and kissed Celia on the cheek. That was an excuse to whisper in her ear without others seeing. "What do you need?" he asked.

"A pair of pants," she whispered. His nose wrinkling, Rich knew why. But he didn't say anything. He simply rose, tucked the book into Celia's backpack, and zipped it up. Then he took off at a trot to the Goodwill trucks, to see if there were any garbage bags of free clothes.

A half hour later he returned, and Celia was still there, reeking. But night had fallen and in the dark he and the other street kids circled Celia so the men in the cars would not see her change. They covered her with their bodies while she stripped and put on the pants Rich had found. They sang silly songs to her to make her feel better. Celia threw the wet jeans into the gutter, where they lay for the rest of the night.

* * *

"I'm going to do something," Celia said to her sister.

Alyssa squinted at her suspiciously, and for the first time Celia saw herself. The two were behind the school. This time they were hiding behind the cafeteria dumpster, in case either Teddy or Mom showed up.

It smelled bad, back here, by the dumpster. Their whole lives smelled bad.

"Here, I brought this for you," Celia said, and handed her sister the book Naomi had given her. Alyssa turned it over, looking bored. Butterflies. "Try it," Celia said, like she was asking her sister to try mashed peas or carrots.

"Why bother?" Alyssa asked, her voice low.

She sounded so much like Celia in that moment that Celia was scared. She couldn't let Alyssa give up hope. Maybe Alyssa blamed her. Just a month ago Alyssa was walking across this blacktop, as pure as the tops of flowers. Now she was hurt, and in some mysterious way this seemed like Celia's fault.

"I just wanted to be a good girl," Celia heard herself say, and Alyssa looked up in shock. "That's all I ever wanted."

"Me, too," Alyssa whispered.

Jerome met Ed at the pasture with the white oak. The piece of fabric still hung from the farmhouse dormer, blowing lightly in the wind. The front door was open. Jerome took that as an invitation for what the two men were about to do.

Ed lifted a stepladder from his truck. He and Jerome carried it under the majestic tree. Ed climbed the ladder and cut the frayed rope with a sharp knife, and the blanket bundle loosened from the tree limb. He passed it down to Jerome, who took it carefully with his one hand, bending slightly with awkwardness.

"A few more weeks, the leaves coming in, you never would have seen it," Ed said, climbing down the ladder.

"I was lucky," Jerome said.

The two men carried the bundle to a soft place under the tree. The rope was tightly embedded in the fabric, so Ed carefully cut it open. "Might as well find out now," he said.

They pulled open the blanket.

There, coiled in years of dark, spotted with the passing rains and dried by the sun, was a collection of artifacts. Jerome knew no other way to describe it. Several nightgowns, tightly coiled. A faded dress. A pair of worn brogans. A rusted brooch. A favorite teacup. Set on top of all this was a photograph of a woman.

Jerome gently lifted the bordered photo. It was a Kalapuya woman standing outside the farmhouse above them. She was wearing a simple farm dress, tight at the waist. Her hair was swept off her neck, and her face was beautiful, with serious eyes and wide cheeks. There was resolve in the full mouth.

Jerome turned the photo over. A note was written on the back, in spidery pen: *Tasmin, remember I kept you safe*.

"That sounds ominous," Ed said.

Jerome looked back at the empty farmhouse. "This whole area is bad. It almost makes me believe in evil spirits."

"People don't need spirits to make them evil," Ed said, surprising Jerome.

"Can I keep ahold of all this?" Jerome asked. "Just for the time being."

"Sure," Ed said, after a moment's hesitation. He wrapped it back up, loosely. "If you don't find her family, I'd like it all. There is so little of us left."

Jerome stretched. He wondered what kind of life the woman had led, living in this farmhouse outside of Elk Crossing. Had her people come from afar, to help her walk on in the traditional way, once her time had come? Maybe more importantly, what had she known about the graveyard, with its row of child graves?

Naomi had been thinking about graves, too. Those bodies hadn't just tumbled themselves into their coffins, she thought, morbidly.

After dropping Jerome at the pasture, she had headed to the Elk Crossing funeral home, named the Crossing Home. It was still open, no doubt until the final population of the town was put to rest. Naomi let herself in the pink building, hearing the chimes ring. She stood in the waiting room, taking in the way the Oregon light poured in the windows. She rang the bell on the counter, sharply. After a time, the funeral director hobbled out, tucking in his shirt with one hand, balancing on his cane with the other.

He was a short, round man who looked to be in his eighties, with a large head and wobbly blue eyes. He had the unkempt look of sin, his cheeks peppered with old beard. His large eyes looked at her, accusingly. His face said nap.

Naomi gave her best country smile and extended her hand. He ignored it, shuffling out with his cane and lowering his wide bottom into a waiting room chair.

"I heard about you," he sniffed after she introduced herself. He was of the generation that looked to the side of young women, as if they were contemptible. "Missus Horn at the courthouse said a lady and a soldier come, inquiring after records. You asked after the graveyard." He gave another self-important sniff.

Outside the windows the white cottonwood blooms drifted, catching on the bushes. "I lived down in Opal," Naomi said. "Used to be cattle country, but nothing left now. There's no place like home, is there?" She added the last with a touch of menace.

His blue eyes caught her. They were cold, filmed inside like a dead baby bird in its shell. Naomi dropped the pretense.

"Have you been the director here for long?" she asked, knowing the answer.

"Fifty years," he croaked, his neck wobbling.

"That's a lot of dead to bury," she said.

He grunted.

"What do you do when you get unidentified bodies?"

The hands on the cane changed somehow. "You mean the Does in the graveyard."

So much for sneaking up to it. "Yes," Naomi said, leaning forward to let him know she was serious.

He didn't answer straightaway. Most people didn't. "I take care of the cemetery. Well, me and Missus Horn. No one left to mow or trim, and that's gotten beyond us. I really shouldn't be taking care of the dead either, to tell the truth." He held up a weak hand. "It's hard work. Physical." He sounded petulant, like a child.

Naomi waited.

"The judge used to call us on those." He took a sudden interest in the floor, rubbing at the old tiles with the bottom of his cane.

"Judge Thurman?"

No answer.

"Judge Thurman is dead and gone," Naomi said. "There is nothing to be afraid of."

His opaque eyes told her otherwise. "There's no statute of limitations for murder, is there?" His voice was as soft as the gossamer strings of white blossoms outside, blowing across the empty parking lot.

"Was it you, or were you an accessory?"

His eyes closed, and Naomi saw sweat appear high on his nose.

It might have been the first sweat of years for him, glossing his cheeks now, too. Maybe those were tears. He put his face against his white hands on the cane. "I stay away from those graves. Sometimes I think they are haunting me. Haunting all of us. Those of us left, anyhow.

"Maybe I should get an attorney," he added.

"I'm not a cop. Invoking counsel won't make me go away."

He glanced at her, terrified.

Naomi suddenly changed tack. "I saw an article about locals who volunteered at the orphanage."

His eyes widened.

"I bet you remember hearing about two little sisters that went missing from that orphanage. Maybe you thought the judge would be calling you about them, too."

There was a deadly silence. He looked dead already, and Naomi had a vision of him on one of his rubber tables. She leaned close enough to feel her cheek warm his unwilling face. She spoke directly to the ghosts in front of him. "One of those girls was me."

"Oh my." His chest began moving, and his hand scrabbled over his cane. His mouth blubbered open, a wet hinge.

"Look at me."

He shook his head. He had hearing aids in his ears, she noticed. Just another human.

"*Look at me.*" Naomi's voice was soft and gentle, and yet so hard. "You can't hide anymore. I'm going to stand on your grave and shout it to the world."

"Please."

"You're old," Naomi said, and the monster was now in her voice.

"You're going to die soon. You will rest with them. The children." She saw him give a shudder.

"There is no absolution," he croaked.

"I know."

He shook his head, rapidly, as if denying that after all this time a truth teller had finally arrived.

"It was the judge," he said. "The judge and . . . his son."

Naomi closed her eyes then. A feeling like the darkest relief swept her. "What was his son's name?" she asked.

Fever. Naomi had the name. Like the malaria and measles, Jerome thought, that once swept the villages of his people, shaking them like acorns from the trees. Like the fire that burns the heart with true love, Ed thought, watching both of them at the table.

They met in the Country Kitten Diner in nearby Murky Grove before heading their separate ways home. The tablecloths were greasy red-and-white-checkered and the special on the blackboard said *Sad Susie*. Jerome ordered it around without knowing what it was, wanting Naomi to stay in the reverie, knowing that was what she needed right now. If you take a burrowing animal and deny it anything but a glass cage, it will break its own claws in the madness to escape. Naomi, who once had no escape, had created one with her mind.

Wesley. Her lips, soundless, formed the word, tried it on, cautiously. It felt okay. *Wesley*, she tried again, her face contorting. Jerome watched, his eyes kind. Ed watched, thinking he was seeing a transmogrification.

Naomi looked up as the waitress was putting down plates. Sad

Susie, Sad Susie, same. It was just stewed vegetables, cooked until limp. "Wesley Thurman," Naomi said clearly, looking brightly around the restaurant as if the world had just awoken and given her a gift. "The man who stole me and my sister is named Wesley Thurman. He kept us in that bunker. He's still alive. He left town after I escaped. But I'm going to find him because he has my sister."

Then, neatly, she began eating, only it was as if she couldn't stop. Jerome wanted to reach, to still her hand, but knew better. They finished their plates and went out to another Oregon spring day. It was the same one that had opened the sky that morning, Jerome knew, only it would always be different. It would get better now, for Naomi.

*   *   *

Sometimes Naomi thought she had a mother. It was a mother she had never met, maybe the one she had always known in her heart had died giving birth to her sister, as the orphanage director had told her. This mother was like an angel. She was out there, floating around, watching Naomi. She was watching Naomi tell Jerome how the funeral director said her sister was not buried in one of the pauper graves. Those were all migrant children. So that meant, Naomi said, that her sister could still be alive.

The ghost of Naomi's mom—maybe—watched as Jerome and Naomi sat in his truck and made a flurry of phone calls, looking for addresses, utility records, credit histories, but it was all smoke and mirrors because Wesley had gone underground. Naomi knew how easy it was to disappear yourself, because this is a big country, full of dark and light. Both she and Jerome had cases where people had created new identities. Naomi had one where a child kidnapper had made a new identity from a Costco card he found on the ground. He had stayed hidden for years that way—until she found him.

There was a part of her that wished she could be one of those people who could read books or watch movies about murder and not even know it was real. But the ghost of her mother knew better.

Naomi knew Wesley was probably good at hiding. But she was better at finding.

It was field trip day. Celia *hated* field trip day. All of downtown was clogged with yellow buses and kids streaming off them, laughing like they owned the fucking world.

Even down in skid row, where she and the other street kids now clustered, the students walked through in groups, their teacher tour guides pointing out the architecture. Celia sat with Rich at the curb, watching. Both of them had the same curdled look on their faces. It was envy and desire at the same time.

"That could be us, Rich," Celia said.

"Well, it's not." His face looked like a bruised pumpkin.

"How old were you when you left school?" she asked.

He turned towards her. "I didn't *leave* school. I was kicked out."

"Why?"

He scratched a leg. "There were some kids. Picking on me." He hesitated, as if he wanted to say more. "I put a firecracker in one of their lockers. You'd have thought I tried to burn down the White House. I got expelled."

"I thought there was some sort of law where they have to educate you. Or something like that."

"Yeah, well, what good have laws done you?"

Celia thought of the jury, their eyes on her.

"So here I am."

Celia decided she had missed part of the story. She watched a group of kids across the street. They looked her age. But they were different. It wasn't just their clothes. It was the way they carried themselves, the way the girls laughed with each other and preened. Everything she questioned they took for granted.

"Did your parents kick you out?" she asked, cautiously.

"You don't understand me. I left."

She made a face at him, appalled. The idea anyone would be on the streets without being forced out made no sense to her.

"I didn't live with my mom," Rich explained. "I was in foster care. My mom lost her parental rights to me. But there aren't enough foster homes, so I had to go to a group home. It was more like a prison. I ran away, and here I am."

"Oh." Across the street, as the kids milled around, their teacher pointed to the turrets above, touching the sky. Celia gazed upwards, too. She was listening to the teacher, following along, pretending to be one of them.

* * *

Once, in fifth grade, Celia had done her class project on butterflies. She had stapled together paper and colored in her own drawings with pencils. She had taken her time and followed the details from the books perfectly. Red admiral, painted lady, peacock. Viceroy.

She had even stolen nail polish from the drugstore to get the metallic sheen just right.

"These are all red butterflies, Celia," said her teacher at the time, Mr. Calhoun. Celia was scared of male teachers. To cover her fear she acted bold.

"Yeah," she told him, and then added sarcastically, "I like the color red. It's bloody."

He had glanced up at her. "Is that a joke?"

"No." Muted now, but the specialness of her book was soiled, touched by his gross fingers. He turned the pages. "You have talent," he had said, with surprise. The next day in class he called on Jessica first—Jessica of the blond hair, the clean neck with a gold necklace around it. Twenty-four carat, Jessica was always boasting. Celia hated her. Then Jessica stood in her white pants and everyone had seen: Celia was not the only red one.

The others had laughed as Jessica bolted from the class, but Celia felt sorry for her. She had followed Jessica to the girls' bathroom, where she was crying. Celia had taken brown paper towels and folded them into long rectangles. "This is what I do," Celia told her. She showed Jessica how to put the homemade liners in her panties.

"Can't you afford pads?" Jessica had asked, and Celia had shaken her head, confused. "That's for when you get your period," Celia had replied. Celia could hear the water dripping in the bathroom sink before Jessica answered: "If you don't have your period yet, why are you bleeding?"

Red butterflies, Celia had thought. Up on the gray ceilings, drinking from the rust-stained sink. Flying in soft red crescents. Landing softer than silk on her arms, stroking the secret softness of her upper arms. Jessica had put the paper towels in her panties. Then the nurse Sally had come, and Jessica got to go home.

Celia had returned to class, to the titter that was now saved for her. Like she had caught the blood. "Do you want to share your project?" Mr. Calhoun had asked in a kind voice, and Celia shook her head, no.

The next day he gave her project back. He had written a big *A* on every single page, ruining it. Celia threw it in a ditch on the way home.

* * *

The scar-faced man hadn't been around for a couple days. Celia hadn't seen Naomi either. The last time she had seen her was the evening Celia pissed her pants and Naomi gave her the book. Celia wanted to talk to Naomi but didn't know how. She thought maybe Naomi could tell her what to do about her sister. She didn't want to leave her sister with Teddy. There was one risk Celia could take, but it might mean losing her sister forever.

Without the scar-faced man around, the streets felt safer. Not that they really were. Celia guessed that was proven true when the next day they pulled another corpse out of the river. It was the girl with the orange hair, and Celia, like all the others, hadn't even noticed she was missing.

The only thing worse than a street birthday, Celia decided, was a street funeral.

It was pathetic, really. All of Celia fought back against the spectacle: a little gathering of the street people outside Sisters of Mercy, a small pile of candles and flowers—which Celia knew would be stolen by morning—on the corner where the girl had often hung out.

"What was her name?" the others asked one another, and someone said she was called Ginger or maybe it was Josie. One boy said she was from Madras, but no one believed him because he was a liar, and the girl with the cell phone offered that once the orange-haired girl said she came from the mountains. Which mountains? No one knew.

Suddenly everyone had been her best friend, and then she was forgotten. This happened in the space of twenty minutes. If Celia died, no one would remember her either.

She sat down next to the candles, scraping wax off the sidewalk with her nails. Rich came and crouched next to her. "Did you know her?" he asked, damp bangs against his forehead.

"Not really," Celia answered, stealing a look at him. "I mean, do any of us know each other?"

"I know you."

"You don't know the worst about me." Celia turned away.

"No. I know the best."

He reached with a cold damp hand. Celia took it.

"Come on," he said, "let's have some fun."

Rich took her on the bus to the outskirts of town, to an area that first looked industrial and then fascinated her when it switched to marshy ditches and ponds. She even saw a man fishing. Finally Rich signaled it was time to get off.

"I don't like surprises," Celia said, like every other abused kid on the planet.

"It's a good surprise," he said, and they stepped off the bus to a warm, curious smell. It took her a moment to realize what it was. Hay. There was something else, too. Celia couldn't place it, but it reminded her of circuses coming to town. Manure, she realized. They walked an empty service road, and then, turning the corner, Celia was astonished to see corrals. Barns. And horses.

"This is the back of the horse track," Rich said, and sure enough, in the distance, Celia could see the corrugated steel of the stands.

For the next dream of a few hours, she got to pet the horses, brush them and touch their velvet noses, see their amazing teeth, giggle at their pendulous bellies. The old Mexican man who worked the stables seemed to know Rich. "I was riding the buses one day, just to stay warm, and saw the track," Rich explained. "I come here to help out when I can."

"You should get a job here," Celia announced, and the old man nodded yes, yes, but Rich shook his head. "I don't even have a diploma," he said, when what he was really thinking was he didn't want to leave Celia all alone on the streets.

"No one needs a diploma to ride a horse," Celia announced, though she never had.

That changed when the old man helped her sit on a stable pony, used to guide the racehorses to the track. The pony felt huge to

Celia, broad-backed and sweet. She sat on his back and closed her eyes and felt the rough hair, the saddle between her legs. Her hands tangled in the mane.

"Celia?" Rich asked after a while.

This, she agreed, was fun.

Naomi put the autopsy photo, given to her by the medical examiner, facedown on the kitchen table. It was out of respect for the sad girl with orange hair and blackened eyes. Once alive, but no longer.

"Didn't the Feds put up surveillance on the docks?" Jerome asked.

"It's been all over the news," Naomi said. "I'm sure he knows better than to return there. He just found someplace else to dump her." She paused. "Her feet show signs of recent use. He's not keeping them as long."

"Do you think it's Wesley taking the street girls?" Jerome asked. It was the first time either of them had voiced the possibility out loud.

Naomi took a deep breath, picked up the cold cup of coffee left on the table. She carried it to the kitchen window overlooking Diane's garden. She thought of all the nonwindows of her captivity.

How she had made windows out of dirt. She thought of Celia and her butterflies.

"The pattern is the same," she said, taking a drink of the bitter coffee. "Children of the forgotten, harvested like the berries of the field."

Jerome winced behind her. He let his face smooth out before she turned.

"I wonder," Naomi said, "what Celia is doing right now."

With Naomi gone from the house, Jerome made a work area on the kitchen table. Diane was out, running errands. Since hearing Naomi and Jerome wanted to stay, she had been a flurry of activity, sewing curtains, finding her old knitting needles. Jerome viewed the knitting with suspicion. He sure hoped Diane didn't expect—

He turned his attention to the photograph from the bundle.

Mary Tarseed. He found her easily enough in the online census. The Tarseed family had been the rare natives who had been allowed to stay when soldiers had forced them off their rich ancestral lands. From what Jerome could gather, Mary's grandfather had been the Elk Crossing town blacksmith, which might have explained why their family was not forced out.

Jerome turned the photo over. *Tasmin, remember I kept you safe.*

One of the census listings showed Mary Tarseed had a toddler daughter, Tasmin. If she was alive, she would now be thirty— his and Naomi's age. But in the next town census—ten years later—Tasmin was not listed. Jerome hoped it was not what he feared.

* * *

Celia was lying on the grass of the waterfront. The girl was motionless, eyes open but unseeing. The clouds passed through the cherry blossom trees above her and speckled her face with shadows.

Naomi sat down under a tree nearby and waited.

Rich, who had led Naomi here, stood behind her, awkwardly. "I can keep an eye on her," Naomi told him, and he shambled away. Naomi could feel the humiliation that followed the boy. To be so alone at such an age.

Celia had taken off her jean jacket. She was wearing a faded blue T-shirt underneath. Her arms were slender, her chest flat. Her hands lay open, relaxed in the grass. Her eyes were unfocused, her cheek against a patch of tiny daisies in the clover. Naomi wondered what Celia was thinking or feeling. Maybe it was just a moment of respite in the middle of the terror. She could see now that Celia was trapped. The streets were a kind of captivity, too.

Celia sat up, and in her eyes Naomi could see the clouds, passing.

Moving slowly, wanting to talk to the girl while she was still in her dreamlike state, Naomi walked over to where Celia sat, her hands soft in the grass.

Lowering herself carefully nearby, Naomi joined her.

"What are you thinking about, Celia?" she asked, her voice gentle.

"The butterfly museum."

Naomi felt her strong thighs press against the velvet of the grass. The world transmitted through her legs reaffirmed her life force. "Tell me about it."

Celia's eyes filled with wonder. "It is a building, out in the country, where there are green hills. It is big, with tall walls and many windows. At the top are skylights, and they keep them polished clean. My mother told me about it."

"Of course," Naomi said.

There was a long pause. Celia was looking away, over the river. Naomi saw the tender heartbeat of her temple. The air seemed to lift around the girl.

"It's a con—conservatory. A living museum. There are full-sized trees in pots, and all sorts of plants. Every room is filled with flowers. There is every kind of plant a butterfly might need for nectar there, and food for the caterpillars, too. There's even humidifiers. To make the air soft."

"For moisture."

"Yes! That's it." Celia's dreamy eyes found Naomi. "You can go room to room there, and each room is filled with butterflies. Sometimes they all take flight, and you can look up to see them flying all together and swirling around the skylights above you. There are more butterflies than you can imagine there. In the butterfly museum."

Naomi could feel her heart aching in her chest.

"Do you want to go there, Celia?"

"Yes. Someday I will go there. I'm going to stand in the middle of the butterflies. I will know then."

"What will you know?"

Celia did not answer. The two sat for a long time. Naomi could see Celia slowly coming back to herself, saw the aching pain in the girl as she woke back to the reality of her life.

Celia blinked. She thought of the dark house she had seen in the industrial area, the boarded-up windows. She felt the eyes behind the window. She wondered if she should tell Naomi about it. But what if Naomi thought Celia was a liar, too? Celia couldn't bear that.

Celia glanced at Naomi. She seemed like she would listen. Celia opened her mouth, but Naomi was standing up, shaking out her legs. Her eyes were on the falling sun.

"I need to go, Celia," Naomi said. "I promise I'll come back, and find you, soon. Will you try and be safe for me?"

Celia nodded.

Rushing through the waterfront back to her car, Naomi saw the small man in round glasses, wearing his fussy suit. He looked like he had been watching her and Celia talk. She felt frustration. Once again the Feds were piddling around when they should be working. The small man watched her hurry past. He smiled at her, as if he were the one judging her.

Naomi walked in to dinner on the table. A lamb chop was sticking up off a plate, a bowl of Jerome's succotash. Diane turned and smiled over a salad she was carrying to the table, and Jerome was at the counter, pouring fresh cider. It was a scene of domesticity that reminded Naomi, sharply, of her years with Mrs. Cottle. The pungent smell of canning spices, the bulbous pickles in the brine on the back porch. A wind swept through the kitchen of her mind, reminding her of all she had lost.

Run, Naomi, said her mind. Run now while you have the time.

Shut up, mind, she responded.

"You're just in time," Diane said, smiling. She looked years younger. Jerome was smiling to himself, as if pleased to see Diane so happy. "Did you have a busy day, dear?"

"I did," Naomi said, taking a seat.

Naomi woke in the middle of the night. Usually this would be from a nightmare, but this time there was nothing. She turned her head to look out the window. Outside a fog hung above the street, sparkling the trees with a thick mist. The moon shadowed behind the clouds. Each of the little branches, Naomi thought, was a hand waving hello.

How had she survived? She knew someplace in her mind was a story. It might be like Celia's butterflies, rich in color, like a children's book. Maybe she had pretended to be someone else, as the woman in the shelter did, making a cape from a pillowcase. She knew she had sung to her sister—she had that knowledge—but the rest of it was gone. Whatever escape hatch Naomi had used had disappeared behind her, and for this she was sad. She would never know how she had survived. The miracle of her own mind was lost to her.

But not for Celia. The girl reminded Naomi of children she had rescued. The ones who survived captivity were the children who had learned to escape into make-believe worlds. Sometimes, later, their parents wanted them to forget these imaginary worlds. They thought that would be a sign of healing—to leave it all behind. Naomi tried to caution such parents. What the children needed, she told them, was to hear they were loved. Not loved despite what happened to them. Loved including it.

That's what we all want, Naomi thought, yawning. She felt the warmth of Jerome next to her and felt herself slide back towards sleep. I must remember to tell my sister that, when I find her.

Celia waited, for the longest time, in the waterfront grass. She had heard Naomi say she would come back.

Dusk fell and night came, and the lawns filled with more street people. Schools of drunks like fish, gasping mouths open as they slumbered, passed out in the grass. A junkie took out his kit right there, in front of Celia. He couldn't hit his arm, so he did his neck, his black bullet eyes on her the whole time he injected the dirty shit.

Still she waited.

Rich came. He was eating an old hoagie sandwich, the kind the corner market sold way past the pull date. A slice of bologna hung out the end like a flap, and Celia could see how the inside was green. His face was at the yellowish point of healing, like a sick banana.

"We should go, this place sucks," Rich said, which was his way of saying it wasn't safe.

Celia didn't want to go. Naomi had said she was coming back.

The junkie had fallen over, the needle still in his neck. Celia wondered if he was dead. Rich ate his sandwich, folding the end of bologna in his mouth. He stood over Celia, watching as the night deepened and the bars closed, ejecting drunks like spawn, and the cars drove by on the ramps above them like Christmas lights, blinking for a party they were not invited to.

"Come on, Celia," Rich said, worried.

From down the waterfront came the sound of hooting, and Rich jumped. Celia could almost smell alcohol on the wind. The jocks might come back. They would come find the junkie. They would find Celia. There were no lights down here. Celia could get beat up like Rich had been. Or worse.

"I don't want to leave," Celia said. "Naomi said she would come back."

She turned her head, peering in the dark, hoping that at any moment Naomi would materialize from the dark, walking with that calm, open look in her eyes.

It didn't happen.

"I want to get the fuck out of here," Rich said, nervously.

Slowly, Celia rose. Her legs had stiffened in the grass. Looking up from the waterfront, they could see groups of young men. Were they friendly? There was no way to know.

Her heart pounding, Celia looked around desperately.

"*Please*, Celia." Rich had his hand out, ready to drag her away.

* * *

"Do you remember telling me about the butterfly museum, Momma?"

It was the next day, and Celia's mother was sitting on the edge of the couch. She was in the place between coming down and needing her next fix, the desperate, sweaty time that would soon drive her to distraction. There really was no good time to talk to an addict, Celia had discovered. They were either high or in withdrawal. Either way they forgot what you said.

"What?" Her mother looked confused. She rubbed a shaking hand over a pale forehead.

"It's not too late," Celia said.

The eyes startled, looked up. Celia could see the fear.

"Not too late for what?" her mother asked, reluctantly.

Celia noticed her hand had left a mark, as though her mom was shrinking inside.

"Too late"—Celia took a deep breath—"to get rid of Teddy. To get clean. Remember how you said you wanted to be a lep—a lepi–lepidopterist?"

Her mother's eyes were on her. They were panicked. The addiction was talking to her, saying, Run away, hide. Cover your tracks. "I never said that."

"Yes, you did!"

"You were too young to remember that."

Celia felt helpless fury. Her mom had just admitted saying it. "Just because you gave up doesn't mean I need to!"

Her mother's eyes teared up. "You're just saying that."

"Teddy hurt me, Mom."

"That's not true. Teddy said—"

"No more, Mom. No more lies. I'm not the liar. Teddy is. The jury was wrong. You were wrong. I told the truth."

Her mother's face looked up at her, white with shock at being told so firmly. Celia could see the guilt rising, all the questions belief would bring. Her own failures as a mother. The face that would stare back in the morning mirror, asking, What did you do? The black call of heroin, not just to soothe the need but to wash away the truth.

"You can still stop, Mom. It's not too late."

"Maybe it is," her mom whispered, looking at the floor.

Celia turned and walked away. She knew she was never coming back.

The inside of the school was the same. The chairs in the front office where she'd sat for lice check were still there. The hallways were empty. Celia had made sure to arrive as school was letting out. Alyssa would be going home, to find their mother more than likely stoned on the couch.

Mrs. Wilkerson looked up from her desk when Celia entered. She no longer looked incredibly old to Celia. She was more like maybe sixty.

"Celia!" Mrs. Wilkerson stopped organizing the papers she had been stacking.

"I'm here for Alyssa," Celia said, unsure.

Mrs. Wilkerson had a broad backside and a reassuring, firm waddle. "She's gone home, sweetie."

"I'm not here to talk to her."

"What is it then?"

"I want to file a report," Celia said.

It felt like the room stopped. *It didn't work before*, the walls said, and almost the same words came from the teacher. Her voice was incredibly kind. "I believe there's a thing called double jeopardy, Celia. You can't try a man twice for the same crime. Even if he was guilty."

Celia closed her eyes. Someone *had* believed her.

"The report isn't for me. It's for my sister."

Mrs. Wilkerson moved quickly around her desk, her hand touching Celia lightly, and then she returned to her chair. "Sit down," she said. She pulled forward a notepad. "How about you start with everything you know."

"Can she go to the same foster home?"

"I can't say, Celia. Child Protective Services makes the decision, but if they think she is in danger, they will remove her. Usually they ask the last foster family if they are willing to take the child back." There was something in her voice that told Celia that Mrs. Wilkerson knew more about the situation than she was allowed to tell. Since she was Alyssa's teacher, she would have met the foster parents when Alyssa was in their home. Celia felt reassured. If Mrs. Wilkerson felt Alyssa would be safe, then Celia would, too.

"Okay," Celia said, breathing deep. She knew that if the family wanted to adopt Alyssa, they could change her name and refuse to let Celia see her. The family could move across the country if they wanted. Celia might lose her sister. Forever.

It was worth it. She began. "She told me."

Celia waited for that night to pass, and another day. Finally she found the girl with the cell phone and offered her the package of

Ding Dongs she was eating as a trade. On the corner, she noticed with a sinking sensation, the scar-faced man was back.

"Mom," Celia said when her mother answered the phone, almost before the first ring was over.

Celia could hear the tears in her voice. "They took her! They came and had her pack a bag and the police were here, too, just in case we tried anything. They arrested Teddy again." Her mother burst into loud sobs.

"What did Alyssa tell them?" Celia asked, calmly, holding the phone and looking at the ebony sky. Little stars out, watching over her sister right now.

"Alyssa asked if they could make her come home, just like you did after the trial, and the officer said no, not after all this. And then Alyssa said Teddy had been raping her, and now I lost both my daughters and *you are never coming back*."

The wind, coming down the street, ruffled Celia's hair and touched her skin, reminding her that right now Alyssa was being tucked into a safe bed, looking out a window, seeing the same stars. The foster family would keep her, and everything Celia had lost would be okay because she had saved the person she loved more than anyone in the world.

Tell her I love her, she wanted to tell those foster parents. Tell her I miss her.

Her mother was crying over the phone. Celia closed her eyes, felt her own tears. Finally her mother stopped. Celia listened to the clicking sound of her mother's ragged breath and remembered so long ago, walking through the meadow. The hands over her eyes, lifting. One, two.

"I'm sorry, Mom," she said, and hung up.

"Why are you saying sorry?" the tall girl asked.

"I don't know," Celia said. "I just am."

The next day Celia fetched her favorite book from the librarian, its pages bulging with drawings. She took one of the stubby pencils from the wood box on the desk and a slip of scrap paper from the stack nearby. Sitting at the table, she closed her eyes to contemplate what she wanted to draw.

She took her time. She paused, her mind tracing the streets. She saw the dark house, remembered the path there. Maybe it meant something. Maybe it meant nothing at all.

After finishing her drawing, she tucked the paper into the middle of the book, between two of her favorite butterfly pictures. She didn't feel relief. The drawing was for herself. No one was coming for her. Long after Celia was gone, floating in a nameless river called time, this paper would be here. A child of the future would open the book and find . . . her.

Find me, she thought.

"There's something bothering you."

Naomi was with Diane, fixing up the bedroom. Diane had made new curtains and gotten a lighter bedspread out of storage in the attic, for the coming summer. It was soft and fresh, with embroidered flowers.

"It's this girl," Naomi confessed, and told her all about Celia.

Diane blinked. "You've been keeping all that to yourself?"

Naomi blushed. She kept a lot inside. It wasn't because she wanted to keep secrets. It just didn't occur to her to share.

"How old is she?" Diane asked, hanging the curtains and stroking them smooth with her hands.

"Twelve, I think." Naomi sounded unsure.

"Parents?"

"I don't know."

Diane's eyes slid away. Her expression said that while Naomi had been trying to find one child, she had abandoned another. Naomi lowered her head.

Diane reached out, patted her arm. "You seem to care about this girl."

"I do."

"Well, help her find her way home."

Naomi turned. Jerome was standing in the doorway, truck keys already in his hand. "I found Tasmin," he said, to Naomi's blank look. "The daughter of Mary, the woman in the tree."

"Now that sounds like a story." Diane chuckled.

* * *

"My mother wanted to keep me safe," Tasmin Tarseed said.

Jerome and Naomi were sitting with her, in front of a campfire. In the distance were rows of rusted boxcars, used as housing for the migrant workers. Clotheslines were strung between the metal boxcars, and from a cracked green hose trickled the only clean water supply. The evening camp held the pure silence of exhaustion. Their work in the berry fields done, the families gathered around the fires, and even usually frisky children sat slack-jawed at the flames.

Tasmin, wearing an orange vest that marked her as an outreach worker, sat politely away from the families. She added another stick to the fire. Her face was ruddy with sun, the smile lines baked in, making her look older than her age, which was thirty. Her black hair was sun-streaked, and she had a restless air about her. Naomi sat comfortably, radiant in the safety of smoke.

"Will you tell us?" Jerome asked, his voice as low as song.

In the distance an owl hooted. Barn, not horned, Naomi thought.

Tasmin nodded. "My mother was concerned. Panicked, more like it. My earliest memory was her coming back from the graveyard, knocking over things in the kitchen—and she was a gentle, careful person. She was muttering something about the children."

She reached for a stick, rubbing moss from it. "I didn't piece it together until later, and by then it was too late. I was too young, you see. Only five. I do remember the tension in town. This one time I went shopping with my mom, and a white man pushed her and called her a drunk Indian. My mother didn't drink, and this puzzled me. Other kids began teasing me, saying my mother was crazy."

Naomi hugged her legs to her chest, wrapping herself in her arms. Jerome looked over at her. "Go on," he told Tasmin.

"It was hard because my mom *was* acting crazy," Tasmin said, guiltily. "What could be crazier than saying you had seen the beloved town judge in the woods, carrying a bound child in his arms?"

Naomi's eyes were wide. She was drinking the truth.

"Did anyone believe her?" Jerome asked, quietly.

"I don't know. I was a little kid. The judge ran the town. It was his berry fields that brought in the money. And it wasn't the local kids dying. Just the odd migrant kid turning up in ditches or the woods. It was easy to blame that on accidents. I remember one they said had drowned. My mom said no one drowns with strangulation marks around their neck."

She put the rubbed stick into the fire. They all watched the flames.

"But then something happened," Tasmin said. "It had to do with the nearby orphanage."

Naomi jerked fully alert, her eyes piercing through the smoke. She stared at Tasmin as the woman went on. "My mother confronted the judge and his son. She got in their faces, said she was going to get a ride to the city—my mother didn't drive, she had never learned—and tell the authorities."

Tasmin took a deep breath. From one of the nearby fires a migrant boy looked over at her. "The Greyhound used to stop in Elk Crossing once a week. One day my mother packed up a suitcase with my clothes. She pinned a note to my shirt. It said my name, and where I was going, which was to my older cousin on the reservation. She sent me away, and I never saw her again. A few days later she died. My cousin said she went back to find out what happened. The judge claimed it was suicide. My mother had been cut ear to ear."

The fire crackled.

Tasmin looked across the campfire. "I went back one summer. The farmhouse was empty, looted by those antique hunters, I guess. Her stuff was gone from her bedroom, too."

Jerome reached into his bag and took out the photograph. Tasmin looked at the picture, turned it over, and read the note in the firelight. She was quiet for a long time.

"I found it in a bundle, tied in the oak tree," Jerome said.

"She wanted me to be the one to find it," Tasmin said. "Will you leave me, now?" she asked, and they did.

He wants to stay hidden, Naomi thought, as nameless as his victims.

She was in her own dream state, standing in the living room. In the kitchen Jerome—frustrated, from the sounds of it—was cleaning her dishes. Naomi reminded herself she had better start picking up more. This wasn't a hotel.

The judge was dead, but Wesley was still alive, and he was here. Naomi could feel it. But Wesley was faceless, just as he wanted to be. Men like him liked to hide. It made them feel bigger to stand in the shadows.

Well, pull him out.

I will, Naomi thought, taking out her phone. Investigations, she thought, were like a ball of yarn. You pulled on one string after another until the whole ball unraveled. And inside, always, was a lost child, arms raised, crying for help.

"Elk Crossing school district," she asked, dreamy. "I know they're closed. I need archives."

Outside birds called. Naomi counted their voices while she waited. Scrub jay. House sparrow. The *tee-yee* of the lesser goldfinch. She began to see the virtue of waking up to the same sounds every morning. It reminded her of her interlude in Opal—because that was what it had always felt like, an interlude between captivity and work, from age nine to eighteen—and how the sweet rhythms of farm life had allowed her and Jerome to grow close. Naomi had learned love and trust. It was astonishing, she reflected, how quickly Mrs. Cottle had taught her just by embodying both herself. And now Diane was trying to do the same.

The phone clicked. She was being transferred. Records were always somewhere. People had a drive to immortalize their past. Even the evil stuff, like Abu Ghraib or the Holocaust. They liked to take pictures, keep journals. Because they believed in what they were doing. No one, Naomi had learned, did evil without believing it was right at the time. Maybe this was why it was nearly impossible to talk them out of it.

Finally the phone connected to the school district offices in Murky Grove, and there she could imagine a woman in a flowered smock—her name was Patty—making her way into a cold basement filled with files. Getting a call from a real-life investigator was about as much excitement as she could stand, Patty said. Naomi reminded herself to send Patty a box of chocolates later. People liked to be thanked like that.

"Thank you, Patty," Naomi said warmly, and hung up.

Jerome was behind her, holding a dishcloth in his one hand. Naomi turned, saw his handsome face. "Sorry about the mess," she said. "We're getting the Elk Crossing yearbook, express mail. We're going to find out what Wesley looks like."

But in her heart she thought she knew.

Later Naomi sat with Jerome on the front porch. It was a cold night, and she wondered again where Celia and the others slept. Behind them the house was dark with silence. Diane usually went to bed early.

Jerome put his arm around her. They always sat like this so Naomi was on his good side—his left—to hold hands or let him touch her. It had already become instinct.

"Tomorrow?" he asked.

"Back downtown," she answered, and she told him Celia's story about the butterfly museum.

"Do you think it's real?" he asked, his voice soft.

"I hope it is, for her sake."

"She'll find something else to believe in if it isn't," he replied. "People with hope are like that."

"I know." She sighed. "I just hope she doesn't have to."

He kissed the top of her head. "Come to bed?"

She leaned against his cheek, felt his warm breath. "Yes."

You didn't come back!"

This, Naomi thought, was not what she had been expecting. Celia, instead of being grateful, was spitting mad. All the rage of her young life was pouring out.

"Well, I'm here now," Naomi said, her back bristling a bit.

They were down on the waterfront, in front of the river. Naomi had found Celia and Rich crossing the footbridge—the other street kids said they usually came that way late mornings after sleeping under an overpass. Naomi felt bad Celia was sleeping in the dirt, and this made her feel guilty, and that made her mad. That along with waiting for hours, from morning until noon, until she finally saw the two figures nonchalantly crossing the bridge. Her relief, like that of a parent who catches her kid playing in the street, was mingled with frustration.

Celia stopped. "Oh. You," she said, sarcastically.

Then they were off. Rich backed away, eyes wide, at the sight of the two of them fighting. Catfight, he knew others would joke. But he could see the pain radiating off both of them. So much disappointment in the world.

"Long time no *see*," Celia said, her eyes mirroring the river.

Naomi knew she should have stopped there, be the adult to the child, but something in her flared, too. "Sorry, I was too busy trying to save you."

"You're not trying to save me or anyone else! All you care about is your sister, and that isn't even about her!"

All the air in the world could not help Naomi then. Her breath froze in her chest.

"You don't even want to save her! You just want to stop feeling guilty, and guess what?" The poison was leaving Celia now, collapsing her into tears. "You can't! She's dead! She probably fucking died or died fucking, years ago, I bet in that house, and you didn't care because *you are too late*."

Naomi tried to breathe.

"No one can save me now." Celia had fallen to her knees, her cheeks red, her face shiny with mucus and tears. "No one can save anyone." Her voice came out dead and remote.

Rich went to lift his friend. He used his loose shirt to wipe her face. The look he gave Naomi was one of reproach. You should have come back, it said.

I'm sorry, Naomi wanted to say, but didn't. Her backbone felt like fire. Rich was walking Celia away, and pretty soon they disappeared up to skid row. Skin row, Naomi remembered a cop calling it once. Like it was funny.

* * *

Celia had escaped to the place before time. Lemon yellow, an ocher like the reddest of hearts. More of them coming now. Sapphire blue, silver tipped. Eyes gazing in astonishment from the backs of wings. Zephyr. Swallow. Long-tails. Creatures longer than history, before the Stone Age. There are fossils of butterflies.

Rich was shaking her, saying, "Hey, Celia." And others were saying "What the fuck" and "Why doesn't she snap out of it." But Celia wasn't there. She could feel the grainy curb outside Sisters of Mercy under her bottom; she could see her limp hands at her side. That didn't matter. She was floating someplace above them all, her arms as light as the wings surrounding her.

Rich led her to the dumpster behind the Greek restaurant, but it was locked, a bright new padlock on it. Rich leaned against it, putting his face on the metal lid and closing his eyes in despair. Celia just stood there. It figured, she thought. It just did.

"Come on," Rich said, leading her by the hand like she was a little child. They went back to the row, and Rich carried her a plate of beans from Sisters of Mercy.

Later Celia climbed tiredly up the hill to the overpass. She lay down in the dirt hollow that knew her body. She hadn't spoken since seeing Naomi that morning.

She felt rather than heard Rich moving in the dark. Slowly, with tenderness, he moved his big body until he was close to her. He reached out, touched her side, felt for her hand. She gave it to him. Rich cradled her hand like it was the most precious gift he had ever been given, and she could hear his breathing in the night.

Closing her eyes, Celia felt the butterflies. Come live, they said, flying all around her. Say you are sorry.

A sweet chariot, swinging low, flickering out of the light. A wide-open feeling. Her sister laughing, toddling across an orphanage yard. A forgotten memory, returning.

Naomi woke. She untangled from Jerome, his naked skin silky against hers. When she had come back yesterday, he had consoled her, and later they had made love under the quilt and Naomi cried afterwards.

Rising quietly, Naomi slipped into her pair of soft cotton pants and a shirt. Going downstairs, she thought of a big breakfast. Bacon, eggs, toast. A pot of coffee strong enough to make your hair curl, laced with plenty of cream and sugar.

Today she had an appointment with Sean Richardson. Then she was going to find Celia. She didn't want anything to happen to the girl.

* * *

Jerome spent some time cleaning up after Naomi left—she had made an effort this time, but boy, she had a long way to go—and called Ed Ashtree, arranging to visit him. Then he went online for a while, fruitlessly searching for any information about Wesley. It appeared the man had dropped off the face of the earth. There was nothing.

The mail slot banged open, and a thick manila envelope dropped through the slot. It landed in the basket Diane used for mail. *Elk Crossing School District, Archives*, the return address said. Patty had added a smiley face to the front.

Setting it down on the kitchen table, Jerome slipped a sharp knife under the flap. The faded red yearbook slid out. ELK CROSSING HIGH, the front said, in crooked gilt lettering.

Jerome sat down, broke the spine, flipped open the yearbook, and began turning the pages.

There. A thumbnail photo. Wesley Thurman. He frowned, remembering what Naomi had told him.

"There's something we'd like to share with you," Agent Richardson said.

Naomi walked into his office. There, sitting in the chair she had once refused, was the scar-faced man. He was wearing a suit.

He rose, holding out a thick hand. His broad face smiled, the scarred seams of his lips moving. "Specialist McConnell," he introduced himself, in a thick, warm brogue.

"Shit," Naomi said.

Specialist McConnell, as he told her, was a field agent from New York. Hearing about these cases, he had offered to come out—he had a sensitivity for work involving street kids, he said. He had been on and off the streets himself when he was growing up. He understood the culture.

The scars? Naomi asked. "I started boxing when I joined the Marines," he said, folding his legs. "Obviously I didn't stop in time. Truth to tell, the scars help in the undercover work. No one believes someone who looks like me is FBI."

"You were following Celia outside the library because you were worried about her?" Naomi asked, swinging her arms restlessly with anger. Not at him. At the sense of dread creeping on.

"I've been worried about her. All of the girls." He paused. "I didn't know who you were, so I thought it best to vamoose when you came running up behind me. Then Agent Richardson told me, and I haven't wanted you to blow my cover."

"Have you found anything out?"

"I've been posing as a john. A creep. Asking around," he explained. "I know all the code, the language. Asking for 'sweet treats.'" He made a disgusted expression with his mouth. "I've gotten a break. Rumors. There is a house where a man takes the girls."

"But no one knows where it is."

He looked over at Richardson. "You were right about her." He turned back to Naomi. "He's hiding in plain sight."

Naomi felt a wave of sickness coming. A generic-looking man who had led a generic-looking life, she remembered having thought scornfully. "Oh no." Naomi almost doubled over with the pain. Her phone pinged, and she reached for it.

It was a message from Jerome, with a picture of the yearbook photo of Wesley Thurman attached. Naomi looked down.

Even as a young man he had looked the same: small and fussy, with round glasses, and shorn hair.

It was Celia's birthday.

After eating, she said good-bye to Rich and then jumped the fence for the Goodwill truck, rummaging through the black plastic bags left by others. She found a fresh pair of boys' jeans, a newish top, and a stained white sweatshirt that said DANCE. She even found new socks, soft and white and pink.

She lugged these treasures up the steps to the library. The scar-faced man was not around, and Celia felt relief. Inside, the elderly librarian said hello.

In the family washroom Celia locked the door, then filled the sink with hot water and hand soap. She stripped, shoving her dirty clothes into the trash can. She washed her pits with their soft beginnings of hair, her tummy, her cloven buttocks, and, last, the place between her legs. She dried off the best she could with the rough paper towels. Finally she doused her head in the now grayish sink, scrubbing her scalp with her nails, and vigorously washed her face.

Drying off with more paper towels, she leaned forward at her reflection.

Her eyes, staring back in the clean mirror, were large and luminous. Her skin, relieved of dirt, was soft and pale, with honey-colored freckles on her cheeks. She touched the thin skin under her eyes, saw the eyebrows, the soft pink of her lips.

She smiled defiantly. Fuck you, Teddy. I am pretty.

She put on the new clothes, enjoying them against her skin. Finally she slipped on her worn shoes, unlocked the door, and ran up the marble stairs, her hand barely touching the rails. Below her the librarian smiled.

The library had a new book about butterflies. Celia was immersed in it, aware of the sun passing over the windows. She was in her favorite chair, where the sun traveled the corner of the building, catching like fire on the tables. Celia felt her breathing slow, turning the pages. She was lost inside the book, seeing herself in a different world—among the butterflies.

"Hello, miss."

She looked up, annoyed. This was the cost of getting clean: every creep would want to talk to her. Instead she was surprised to see a small man with round glasses. It took her a moment to place him. He was the one who had helped her that night someone spiked her drink.

"Hey," she replied with cold caution.

"Mind if I sit?" He flashed a smile at her and signaled at the chair opposite her. Between them the table gleamed.

Celia shrugged. She could always get up and move if he bothered her.

He had a book and soon opened it, reading across from her. Celia snuck a glance, her own concentration broken. It was something about police work. She saw his silver hair, cut short on the sides, just like a cop. A flash of understanding came to her. This was the undercover man Naomi had mentioned! Relieved, she returned to her own book, wiggling a little in her chair, pleased she had figured it out.

The clock ticked. The sun was behind clouds. Celia kept sneaking glances at the man, but he seemed immersed in his book. For some reason, he looked mildly put out, and this caught at her. Gave her a tug.

"Are you . . . studying?" she asked.

He gave her a curt nod and turned a page.

She yawned and put her book down. Getting clean made her sleepy. She wished there was a place she could lie down for a nap.

"Tired?" the man asked. It was hard to see his eyes behind his glasses.

"It's not a big deal," Celia bragged.

"What are you up to today?" he asked indifferently, as if it didn't matter.

"It's my birthday," Celia said, proudly, and then added, "I'm going to find my friend Naomi later. I bet you know her."

"I bet I do."

"I'm going to help her."

"Help her what?"

"Find her sister."

"And how are you going to do that?"

"I think I know where her sister might be."

"Oh." The small man put down the book. Now she could see his blue eyes behind the glasses. They were grave and—what was it? Worried. No, Celia told herself. Not worried. It was respect, for her. "And where would her sister be?" he asked.

"I saw this house. In the industrial area."

Now the face was still. The blue eyes were on her, watching.

"I saw it a while ago," Celia said. "There was someone inside, watching me. I think it might be the man who is taking the girls. I bet he took Naomi's sister, too. That's where she's at, and I'm going to help Naomi get her."

The small man spoke slowly, carefully, like her answer mattered. "Did you tell Naomi where this house was?"

She saw an edge of his narrow teeth—she was surprised they weren't nicer. "No." She shook her head, embarrassed. "I was going to, only . . ." She trailed off.

She didn't think the undercover man would understand what it was like to be told your entire life you were a liar. How after a while you started believing no one would ever believe you, and maybe you even stopped believing yourself.

But he was smiling. It was okay after all.

"You can show me," he offered.

They walked down the wide marble stairs, and below them the librarian looked up to see Celia leaving with an older man in a suit. The man looked professional, but all the same, the librarian frowned. She swallowed her instinct to say something, to call out. She wasn't sure why.

Above them the sky was a clear blue, with fluffy white clouds.

"It's pretty, isn't it?" He smiled. "Just like you."

"How long have you known Naomi?" Celia asked and, just for a second, caught a passing look of surprise on his face.

"Oh, I've known her . . . forever." He smiled to himself.

"Really?"

He asked, slyly, "Do you know what I do?"

"You're undercover," Celia answered, proudly. In the blocks below them was skid row. Her friends would be there, and the strip clubs, the gay bars. But the streets were empty here, and besides passing the corner market, they would stay empty until she showed him the boarded-up house. Celia felt a small sense of disquiet at that, but she told herself he was okay; he was like Naomi: a good guy.

"See that store up there?" he asked, pointing at the corner market.

Celia nodded.

"I'll buy you a soda. You can drink it on the way. You like black cherry cream, right?"

"How do you know that?" she asked, slowing.

"That night we met, remember? That's what you were drinking."

"Oh."

Celia really didn't want the soda. She wanted to show the man the scary house so Naomi would be impressed. She would find out Celia was a nice girl after all.

"I thought I told you, you ought to be careful what you drink on the streets."

Celia remembered him handing her the soda outside the store, the top already opened. Watching her, carefully, as she drank it.

They were outside the house. The blank boarded-up eyes of the windows, tufted with blankets, stared back with horror at her. Her limbs felt numb. Celia watched one eye become five become nothing. She was whirling. She saw his teeth: narrow, edged in dark. She was falling.

"I got you," he said.

* * *

Naomi came sprinting down to skid row. "Have you seen Celia?" She stopped, leaning over, panting, asking Rich.

Rich was on the corner, panhandling. "She said she was going to the library," he said.

"I was just there," Naomi said. The librarian said Celia had left with a man in a suit. Naomi had shown her the picture of a younger Wesley on her phone, and the librarian said yes, that was him.

Naomi felt pure, unadulterated panic. Nothing in her recent life had felt like this. Rich, his own thighs tingling with fear, was unable to speak.

"You looking for Celia?" It was the girl with the phone. "I saw her a little bit ago. She was in the corner market."

"Was she with anyone?"

"Some dude in glasses." The girl shrugged, chewed a hangnail.

Naomi ran to the corner market. Inside, the clerk shrugged. Outside, Naomi spun around in a circle.

Celia was gone.

THREE

—

BUTTERFLY

In the basement of every house there was an urn. It was the bowl of water he gave her to wash her face. It was the toilet that had to be flushed with the waiting buckets. It was something more: love in the night.

Sarah liked the basement because she could catch a glimpse of the world outside the barricaded windows. Sometimes she touched the boards nailed over the window—lightly, because Wesley had told her he could see and hear everything she did. Sometimes she thought Wesley crawled inside her skin and saw through her eyes. But no. That was too scary to be true.

In the basement Sarah could talk to Little Self. Little Self lived under Sarah's armpit. She hid under the skin between her rib and her rushing heart, where Wesley could not see or hear her. When Sarah was alone, Little Self came out, scampered down her arm, and Sarah opened her hand so Little could perch in her palm and they could talk.

The dirt floor of the basement was spotted with blood. Wesley did that. He said he would do it to Sarah, but she didn't think so, though she didn't know for sure.

He has the girl I saw outside, Sarah told Little Self. He put her in the room, Sarah said, her lips moving silently.

Little Self shook her tiny head. This was bad. This was worse than bad.

Sarah had seen the girl outside through the window before. She had short curly hair and was just standing there, staring at the house. Sarah had wanted to yell, Run away! Run now! Before he catches you! But now it was too late.

You need to leave now, Little Self said. She often told Sarah to escape. But the last time Sarah had tried, Wesley had hurt her real bad. It had taken her forever to mend, and now one of her ankles was twisted forever. If she tried to run, she would not get far.

I'm waiting for Big Sister, Sarah mouthed.

You can't wait anymore, Little Self announced.

Big Sister said she would come back for me, Sarah replied stubbornly.

Sarah wanted Big Sister to come back. She was scared. She had no idea what that world out there might be like. It might be full of worse men than Wesley. There might be giant monsters out there who would eat her, tear her skin from her bones.

You need to—

There was a sound on the wooden basement steps behind her, and all the spit in Sarah's mouth dried up. She closed her hand, and Little Self scampered up her arm, ran under her armpit, and burrowed into her skin next to the noisy blood of her heart. There she curled into a tight ball so she wouldn't have to hear or look at Wesley.

Sarah heard his rough voice behind her. No matter how long it had been, just the sound of Wesley's voice was enough to make Sarah's legs watery with fear. She closed her eyes and, turning around, forced herself to see him in the only way she could.

* * *

Celia didn't open her eyes at first. A smell came over her, like a formaldehyde she had never known. Dried liquid, crystalline on her cheeks. Dim memories of a forgotten place before it all. Can you dream what you don't know?

Celia's eyes opened.

* * *

Wesley was sitting, hunched, at the kitchen table, eating. There was only one chair, and Wesley was the only one allowed to use it. His short silver hair shone in the lamplight. Inside one of the hall closets he kept the suits and shoes he wore when he went out. When he returned he took his street costume off, put on old pants and a dirty shirt. Like a boogeyman.

Baked beans were the only thing on the plate in front of him.

He scraped the plate with his fork and ate. He looked at Sarah standing in the corner. She made sure he could look through her, and that her hands were hanging like bags of meat at her side.

Wesley had brought Sarah to this house when she was small. He put something over her head and put her in the back of something that bumped, and she threw up inside the cloth. When she had gotten bigger, Wesley had started leaving and finding others. He didn't keep them very long, and lately he didn't keep them hardly at all.

He would have gotten rid of Sarah, too, if he weren't trying to punish her sister for leaving. He did that by keeping Sarah alive.

Then the beans were gone. He stood up, dunked the plate and fork in the plastic bin full of cold gray water. "Wash this," he ordered her before going back upstairs.

Sarah was back in the kitchen. Put crackers on a plate, Wesley had told her.

Wesley didn't know Sarah had thoughts. He thought she was dumb. That's what he said. Dumb as a post. Not like her big sister, who was the only one smart enough to escape. Sarah could tell Wesley hated that—he talked about her sister with hate—and yet he seemed to respect her, too.

Wesley didn't know about Little Self, or that at night she peeked out, looked around to check all was safe, and climbed carefully onto Sarah's chest to protect her. Now, in the kitchen, Sarah held her arm straight out and watched Little Self slide down to land, triumphantly, in her open palm.

Look, Little Self told her.

Sarah looked around. The counters were covered with cans and boxes, kerosene for the lamps, big jugs of water that glimmered in the dark, and a hot plate for Wesley to heat his food. There was nothing sharp in the kitchen. The only metal was dull butter knives and forks. On the edge of the counter was a small locked box. That was where Wesley kept his gun.

No, not that, Little said.

Sarah looked around again, saw a box of rat poison in the back of the mess. Wesley put the little pellets around the house and Sarah found the rat bodies later, dried up and tiny at the waist. Sarah shook her head. So many times she had wanted to die but not here. She wanted to die on the outside. She wanted to die feeling free.

Sarah looked at her soft feet on the dirty floor. The toes looked boneless. The twisted ankle hurt. She looked back at Little, perched in her palm. Little had hard feet that could run. Little had legs that could stretch. Not Sarah.

I'm afraid, Sarah told her.

Little Self shook her head. You need to leave *soon*.

She climbed up Sarah's arm and burrowed back into her armpit. When Sarah put the crackers on the plate, she heard crying.

In the courthouse downtown Naomi and Jerome found records of the trial against Celia's stepdad. They located Alyssa's foster parents, unraveled the rotten core of Celia's story until Jerome landed outside Teddy's jail cell, where he was again awaiting trial, this time for raping Alyssa.

Teddy, greasy in his jail jumpsuit, had no answers. The defense attorney sat nearby, in the plastic chair. He was there to make sure Jerome didn't ask Teddy about his crimes. That was their deal. Jerome could only ask if Teddy knew where Celia might be, or knew anything about the man who had taken her. As if pedophiles had a secret grapevine. Jerome thought of the games he used to play with Naomi as kids, making phones with two orange juice cans and string, talking from room to room.

Teddy didn't know anything. "Sorry I can't help you, brother," he said, as if they were kin, and Jerome wanted to spit in his face.

* * *

After long hours of searching, Naomi fell apart, sobbing on a street corner. "We have to find her," she kept saying, and Jerome noticed that for all of Naomi's determination to find her sister, it was this homeless child that had sparked the terror.

Jerome held her with his one arm, wishing he had two.

Do you have any idea where she might be?

No, said Mrs. Wilkerson, tears in her eyes as she passed them an old school photograph of Celia. Naomi had filed a missing persons report and was making flyers.

No, said Alyssa, trembling between her foster parents, each holding one of her hands in their laps.

No, said Rich and the others. No, said the nuns at Sisters of Mercy. No, said the manager at Aspire, turning her head into the locker to weep. No, said everyone they asked on skid row, until at long last Naomi turned a corner a week after Celia went missing, and a junkie scratching his neck said he had never heard of the girl.

Even now, more than ever, the butterflies came. They blanketed Celia in the darkest night. They filled the foulness and beat back the air. The ceiling was not a ceiling; the room had no doors. The butterflies kept Celia from asking the wrong kinds of questions, the questions that would unlock the scream of panic from her throat. They told her, *It's nothing*, and *Let's focus on that window*. They told her, *Shhhh*, and they covered her face with their glowing beauty when the pain got too much. Nothing, not even he, could penetrate her glory.

But sometimes the predators come no matter how hard you try. They want to pin you down. They want to kill you. Celia knew that's what he planned to do. *Shhhh*, said the butterflies, filling the room. Think only of your escape.

When she got ahold of herself, Celia let the butterflies carry her gently back down to earth—and she watched the young woman who came with the food.

The young woman was ageless, her face like plastic stretched to some unseemly point. She had eyes that turned inwards. She came in twice a day, first turning the deadbolts from the outside. She brought crackers on a plate. *I am looking for my sister*, the flyer had said. *She is about twenty-five.*

The young woman handed her a dirty towel, her face mute. Celia wiped blood off her chin. The towel smelled impossibly bad, like it had never been washed. Someplace in this horrible house, Wesley breathed. Celia could feel his dragon breath from afar.

Her name is Sarah, Naomi had said.

This, Celia thought, is Naomi's sister. They even looked alike.

Looking over her shoulder, Sarah held her left arm out. She opened her palm. Rising from her corner, Celia carefully, painfully, hobbled close. Celia opened her mouth to speak, but Sarah shook her head. Wesley might hear them. So instead Celia tilted her own head, in question. Is there something there I should see?

Sarah nodded, eagerly.

Celia looked into the empty palm.

Tell her I miss her. Celia remembered the flyer. *Tell her I am sorry.*

Celia opened her mouth and stopped. Be careful, something inside warned her. She might not be ready.

Together they peered into the palm. Sarah's lips moved. She was talking to whatever was there. Celia closed her eyes in relief. She knows she is in hell, she thought, and if she knows that, she wants to escape.

At nights Wesley locked Sarah in the closet. Little Self liked it there. She climbed the metal rod above Sarah, swinging upside down above her. Sometimes she sang the same songs Sarah's big sister had sung so long ago. The best one was about a sweet chariot. Sarah didn't know what that meant except her sister was coming back. It was taking a long time.

The girl reminds you of Big Sister, doesn't she? Little said.

Yes! Sarah breathed, sleep filling her. She does.

Stay awake, Sarah. You have to think.

Think about what? Sarah asked, fearful.

How to escape, Little said. You have to take the girl with you. She can show you the outside. Ask for her help. You can find your sister out there.

He said he will keep me forever, Sarah's lips murmured.

No. It is time. Before he—

Yes, Sarah breathed out, her eyes closing.

* * *

After about a week, Celia had, miraculously, found a way to talk to Sarah. She did it without making any sound. Sarah was remarkably good at reading lips. Sarah had learned to read lips from watching Wesley. It was easier, and better, than looking in his eyes.

The cracker plate was on the dirty floor between them. Wesley was somewhere in the house. It was enough to make a breath drop with fear.

Sarah smiled at Celia, showing a line of teeth pebbled from neglect. Celia felt sorry for her, seeing those teeth, feeling this house. What a tender heart Sarah must have—as scared as any street kid. Sarah looked over her shoulder, held her left arm out again, and opened the palm. Celia stepped closer and carefully put her arm around Sarah's waist. The flesh was soft, and at first stiffened in fear and surprise. Then it softened.

Little Self wants us to leave, Sarah's lips moved.

I will help you, Celia answered, her heart rising with hope.

One window in the basement, Sarah said. That's where I saw you.

That was you! Celia was astonished. I thought—

Don't say his name.

But how can we get out? He is always watching.

Sarah frowned, thinking.

I have an idea, Little Self said from Sarah's palm.

You left me, her sister was saying, whispering down an empty street. *You left me and you left her.*

Naomi woke with a start. The night was wet outside her window. The foul hours of dawn, she remembered a fellow survivor saying. The time when those in pain remember. The knowledge that tomorrow has brought yesterday back.

Her mind was grainy with lack of sleep. Next to her Jerome was in the deep, soundless slumber of the exhausted. His gun holster was slung over the armchair. Naomi remembered Diane laughing when they first met, outside the courtroom where they were both testifying.

Her sister had been about to say something else in the dream. Naomi turned to the window. No, it was Celia. Naomi winced as she remembered that last, explosive talk, the child's cheeks lathered with tears. Celia had been saying something Naomi hadn't wanted to hear. But she did now.

"You can't! She's dead!" Celia had yelled. "She probably fucking died or died fucking, years ago, I bet in that house, and you didn't care because you are too late."

I bet in that house.

Oh my God, Naomi thought, sitting straight up.

"Celia knew where the house was," Naomi told the gathered men.

They were sitting around Winfield's desk. Sean Richardson was there, and so was Specialist McConnell. It was very early morning, and they all looked sleep deprived. A row of takeout coffee cups circled the desk. Naomi had bitten hers.

"The question"—Winfield cleared his voice—"is how we find out what Celia knew."

"We've talked to all her friends," Jerome said. "None of them know anything. That boy Rich is beside himself with worry."

"What did she tell you again, Naomi? *That house.*" Specialist McConnell spoke in his warm brogue. "Nothing more?"

Naomi shook her head, sick with herself for not asking when Celia had told her.

"What about her mom?" Sean Richardson asked.

Everyone had read the court transcripts. The trial had been a travesty. "Celia the liar." That the judge had allowed the jury to hear this still inflamed Naomi. Of course Teddy was going to call her a liar—she was speaking the truth.

Jerome had done an interview with Celia's mother because Naomi didn't think she could handle it. "She's in a treatment center. She says that losing both Celia and Alyssa made her get clean. I don't know what to think. But she doesn't know anything."

"It seems like Celia didn't tell anyone where this house was," Richardson said.

"She told someone," Naomi replied obstinately.

"How do you know that?" Richardson asked, respectfully.

"It's like the fairy tales," Naomi said, remembering her other missing child cases. "Celia was trapped and lost, alone in the wilderness. She will have left a trail of crumbs somewhere. All children do."

"Then let's find the trail," Winfield said, ending the meeting.

Jerome stood outside next to his truck with Naomi. He wanted to drive down to the reservation. If there was the smallest chance the cousin who had raised Tasmin Tarseed knew anything about Wesley, he wanted to find it. "Will you be okay?" he asked, as if he were leaving for a week and not just a day.

Naomi didn't say anything. Instead she pushed at him with her mind: *Go, help me find her.*

Jerome found Ed in the reservation library, small and overly warm, in a clapboard building. The parking lot outside was almost empty.

"You still got that bundle?" Ed asked, sorting books.

"I gave the photo to Tasmin Tarseed. That's the daughter of the woman whose picture it was. She lived in that farmhouse. Her older cousin still lives here."

"Mrs. Tarseed? Tell her she's got fines." He chuckled.

"Naomi's little friend is missing. A street girl by the name of Celia."

Ed's entire demeanor changed. The two men walked out of the

building. Moss hung off the stunted trees, and mist coiled around their feet. Ed poured strong coffee from his thermos, which once said OREGON DUCKS on it, most of the letters worn off. He passed Jerome the lid cup, and he took a swallow. The coffee was strong and sweet, and tasted like birdsong.

"I'm here to see if there is anything her cousin might know, about where Wesley Thurman went," Jerome explained. "My heart is breaking watching my wife right now. She thinks it's her fault that Celia has gone missing."

"Does she know it isn't?"

"I don't think that matters to her." Jerome handed back the cup, and Ed finished the coffee, screwing the cup back on the thermos. Jerome dug in his jacket pocket, the empty sleeve brushing against Ed. "Pardon my sleeve," he said. He pulled a slip of paper out of his pocket, and Ed smiled. Notes. "This is the address I found." He showed it to Ed, and Ed gave him quick directions. Once in the mountains, Jerome knew, his GPS would chirp off.

His truck bouncing up spring-washed roads, Jerome found the house. It was low and ramshackle, a series of rooflines like the sky. In a pen was a shaggy pony, its hooves split from neglect. At the door was an older woman, curious and waiting. Jerome turned to her as though he had known her his entire life.

* * *

Spring rains lashed the windows. Cousin Tarseed made a living by collecting wild salal to sell to florists. It was hard work, she said, showing her leathery hands. The beds of her nails were stained an eerie fluorescent green. "Looks like I got moss for hands, doesn't it?" she asked, and then grew serious. "I was a bookkeeper once. But the economy went south, so now I live in the mountains and cut salal."

The blanket was open, the tender belongings of Mary Tarseed spread across the table. The cousin thought she would like to keep the teacup for herself, give the rest to the tribe. "I liked Mary," she said. "She was hardheaded. That doesn't do for a woman, most of the time." She sat in her chair, primly, green hands folded in her soft lap. "She shouldn't have taken on that judge."

"So you heard about all that?" Jerome asked, brushing his hair from his eyes.

"Of course! I practically raised Tasmin. It was all she could talk about for ages. But then she stopped. Once she got big enough, she went away to university. She comes home on occasion—works for one of those migrant labor outfitters." She gave a brief laugh that faltered. "I ought to get her into the salal business. They sure work us hard."

"I'm wondering if there is anything you ever heard—anything at all—having to do with the judge's son, and where he might have ended up."

Her eyes met his. She waved a green hand. "All I know is what I heard. I will repeat it for you."

"Okay," Jerome said, and she began.

It was the judge who had gotten the praise, Mrs. Tarseed said. Owner of the Thurman Family Strawberry Farm, big and bluff with those grandfatherly eyes. Imposing on the bench—she had seen him once, while visiting her cousin before she died, and he had been kind to her, waiving a speeding ticket she had gotten out of town. No one had paid much attention to Wesley, small and priggish. He had a sniveling way about him that would have led to teasing had he not been the judge's son. As he got older, he was the one who fixed the problems with the reluctant migrant workers, cajoling and threatening in turn. If a child's body turned up every now and then, it was easy to chalk it up to field accidents. Especially when the son of the judge also began to make a name for himself doing good works. Like volunteering at the orphanage.

The year her cousin died, there had been a restlessness in the town. The people were starting to suspect. They could *feel* it, Cousin Tarseed said. But they went on with their town parade, a festive march of children on Main Street, pulling their Radio Flyer wagons decorated with flowers. It was the height of strawberry season, and the air was filled with their rotting scent. That was the last time she had been in town, trying to recover her cousin's remains, hoping their ancestors had walked her home.

Around that time, Mrs. Tarseed said, there was talk of two sisters gone missing from the orphanage. That got the town's attention. The evil was moving closer to home; it was crawling up their doorsteps in the middle of the night. There were now hushed conversations on sidewalks, quiet as the judge and his son walked up. The judge was aging, and maybe in their secret hearts the townspeople thought whatever was happening would die with him. Instead they now had Wesley and his stove-dial eyes.

The judge passed away and was duly cremated. The bodies stopped appearing in the fields. Maybe because Wesley kept what his father had thrown away. The town swallowed their fears of the missing sisters. They didn't want to think about the graves or the memory of the judge, so complacent in his chair. The last Mrs. Tarseed had heard, Wesley had left town himself. By then most of the people around had either died or moved away.

"What about a mother?" Jerome asked as the story concluded. The rain had stopped. "Didn't Wesley have a mother?"

"Oh, her," Mrs. Tarseed answered. Her green hands suddenly clenched in her lap, as if grabbing a bough. "The story was she left the judge, long ago. Divorced and went to the city and died there. They say she lived in some awful house."

It was then that Jerome knew just what to do.

"What was her maiden name?" he asked.

Rushing back to the city, Jerome saw the coming night sky as he parked by the downtown courthouse, moments before closing. The sheriff deputies frowned at him, hurrying through the metal detectors, until he mentioned their boss by name. Darting up the stairs, proud that he could balance so well even after missing an arm, Jerome bounded up all the flights and sprinted down the echoing hallway of the top floor until he came to the door at the back.

PROBATE, it said.

He ran in to find a lonesome clerk, ready to close for the night. "I need a copy of a will," Jerome breathed, and gave them the mother's name. "It is going to have an address I need."

Wesley was at the kitchen table of what was once his mother's house, eating baked beans again, this time with a tuna sandwich.

After Naomi had escaped when she was nine, he had brought Sarah here. It had been easier to disappear than he would have assumed, just as it had been easy to take children. He had survived on the proceeds of selling his father's strawberry fields and the family home, and when he needed a last name to use, he used his mother's maiden name. He lived a subterranean life, surprised at how quickly time passed even when you didn't have much of anything to do besides dream in the vast expanse between murder and hate.

It had been twenty years since Naomi's escape, he had realized when he saw the flyers around skid row. A woman looking for her sister. The details were clear. Naomi had not only tracked him to the city; she had, in the interlude, become an investigator specializing in finding children like herself.

Yet he hadn't worried. He didn't worry for the same reason he didn't worry about all the girls he had taken over the years. No one had ever stopped him. Or his father.

In his earliest memory he was playing with his father's gavel on the bench, wondering why it was called a bench and not a desk. In the chambers nearby—which looked like just a plain office to him—the door was closed, and his dad was doing something in there to a child around his own age. The gavel was warm and smooth and had heft in his own hand. He remembered holding it, seeing the way the light came in the windows, and had the sudden realization that he might never figure himself out. From the other room came sounds he did not want to hear.

Soon after that, his mother left and his father began building something deep in the woods behind the strawberry fields. No one was allowed to go back there, and young Wesley wasn't sure they would have been able to find it, anyhow. One day he had followed his dad without his dad knowing it. But his father, dressed in the worn trousers and baggy shirt he wore away from the bench, had acted like it was okay. *"You will come to like it,"* he had said.

Now Wesley looked at Sarah, moony-eyed in the kitchen corner. There was something about her that was different. A beacon of light shone from the top of her head and pierced all the floors and the roof above, shooting straight into the sky.

He shook his head, scraped the plate. When he looked in the mirror in the hallway closet and put on his courtroom suit, there was no reflection he could discern. That was the most terrifying idea of all: that it had all been for nothing.

"These taste too sweet," he complained. He looked at the bag of sugar on the counter. "Did you put something in them when I went to piss?"

Sarah looked at him, her eyes blank.

"Stupid." He shook his head again, finished the meal.

The cramps started a few minutes later.

The deadbolts turned. Sarah gestured at Celia. It was time to go.

Wesley was crawling across the kitchen, trying to reach the water. Foam covered his lips. His fingers were wet from making himself vomit, and Celia saw the trail of regurgitated food he was sliding through. They didn't have much time.

Passing, Sarah stepped in his waste, felt it against her toes. He looked up, gasping. She limped past, cringing with fear. His hands grabbed at her twisted ankle as she hobbled by. She reached beyond the empty rat poison box hidden behind the cold gray dishwater tub and found a butter knife.

Hurry, said the butterflies. Celia ran down the basement stairs and Sarah limped, following. Celia tried pulling off the board with her bare fingers. It was too tight. Celia turned to Sarah, her face a white blotch of terror.

Above them, in the kitchen, they could hear Wesley. A gushing sound like water pouring. More vomiting. A crash of metal on the floor. The gun box.

Sarah passed her the dull knife. Celia put it between the board and window and pulled as hard as she could, crying with effort. The wood complained as the nails began to lift. One nail, two, three—

Then a sound on the steps behind them.

Wesley was coming.

Naomi was in the library. She could feel Celia in every room. The marble staircase, without her eager steps racing to the bookshelves. The reading room, where the empty chair mocked Naomi.

"She talked about a house," Naomi told the elderly librarian. Behind her was a new flyer, this one for Celia. Naomi had added the school photo she and Jerome had gotten from Mrs. Wilkerson. Celia looked impossibly young in the picture.

The librarian frowned. Naomi felt she was forgetting something.

"She didn't say anything to me," the librarian said. "I only ever talked to her about books."

"You were kind to her."

"Well, why not?" The voice was peevish, full of guilt. The feeling was stronger. Yes, Naomi was forgetting something.

"It can't be your fault," Naomi told her.

"Why shouldn't it be? Why can't it be all our faults?"

Naomi turned, ready to leave. She looked up at the marble staircase and remembered her first glimpse of Celia, coming down the stairs, holding a thick book in her hand. The cover was dull blue, the edges of the pages silvered. It was a place Celia hid inside. A place where she confided her secrets. A place she filled with sketches.

She turned back.

"Do you still have Celia's favorite book back there?"

The librarian reached under the counter and handed it over.

Sitting down at one of the tables, Naomi opened the book. Scraps of paper fluttered out. Naomi saw drawings of butterflies but also faces and places. She opened one and saw herself. She was smiling in the sketch, her head surrounded with butterflies.

Tucked in the middle of the book was a piece of paper folded tight and tucked between two color plates. Naomi unfolded it. Thick pencil had been applied carefully.

It was a map.

Downtown, the careful script read, and at the heart of the map was the industrial area near skid row. In the middle was a house, with *X*s over the windows and a gate over the door. Under the house Celia had written *Here*.

Celia had oriented it with the one landmark anyone would understand: *River*.

Naomi spun the map. North, you are here. South, you are leaving now. Grabbing the paper, running out the door, panic under your once soft feet, healed and now strong.

She didn't bother going for her car. She ran.

The empty streets became the fields Naomi ran once in escape, now in pursuit. She was turning around in the past, running backwards to what she had feared and lost. She felt the air fill her chest. She felt the strength in her legs.

Deep in the industrial district, Naomi knew she was getting close. She had not seen anyone for blocks. She paused, opened the map, and oriented herself.

The house rose out of the gray landscape like a foul toadstool. The sky above was slate, the sun frightened behind darkening clouds. The windows were all boarded-up, and the door covered with locks. The only window that looked even faintly breachable was at the basement level. A sliver of light showed at the side of the boards. The light was warm and golden. Naomi instinctually recognized the lamplight of her captivity. No electricity, she thought.

From inside, a dim scream. Naomi knew that voice.

Celia.

Without hesitating, Naomi ran up next to the house and, rolling down on the dank soil, in one smooth motion drew her knees back and kicked hard. Glass shattered, a board crumpled, and chunks flew as her feet busted in.

She heard a cry of alarm, and then she was flipping on her belly and dropping in, sightless, before she could even see the ground, before anyone had time to react. She could feel the cool air around, felt her eyes open and her feet willing to find the floor.

She went in with only what she knew: her hands, her heart, her wild fists.

Landing on the dirt floor, Naomi saw, instantly, Celia, shrinking with terror. A defunct oil heater. Sour dirt and the deep, hopeless smell of death.

Wesley Thurman, his silver hair somehow dimmer inside, was holding a gun. He was wearing dirty trousers and an untucked shirt, soaking wet at the chest. He looked completely different from the man she had seen in the fussy suit, as if he had shed a skin and become his own truth. Naomi recognized this Wesley. He looked at her with the vicious temperament of a dog that has only learned to bite. All the hollowness of evil. The sadness.

Cowering in front of Wesley was a young woman. She had brown hair, like Naomi. A wide face, unmarked with time. The sun had never shone on it. The moon only knew it in eclipse. Two wide hazel eyes.

Her sister. This was Sarah. Her sister was in front of her. Naomi saw her bare toes in the bloodstained dirt. She saw a bent ankle.

Sarah tilted her head and stared at Naomi.

Naomi suddenly saw the two of them in a room with the puppy wallpaper. Naomi tucking her baby sister into a crib as the branches traced the window. Singing her the lullabies their mother had sung, songs only a big sister could know. The creak of a step behind them, and a young man coming into the room holding a cloth in his hand.

Wesley pointed the gun at Naomi.

Celia opened her mouth to give warning. Her hands rose, as if to protect Naomi.

But Naomi stood frozen. She saw herself running, forever running, across a night field, the sickness in her that she was leaving her sister behind, that her life had grown so terrible she could knowingly make this sacrifice.

She had known. She had known all along.

"I am so sorry," Naomi said, gutted with pain.

Celia cried in alarm as Wesley shot Naomi.

* * *

Celia yelled. It was a guttural cry, a howl of a childhood lost. Naomi was still standing, a look of white surprise in her face, her hand holding her hip, looking down at a bloom of blood.

Wesley held the gun, hot in his hand. It had been so long since he had fired it. The feeling brought back memories better left un-examined. His dad, looking up from the freshly built trapdoor, the smile on his face as hollow as a fly landing on a sill. He remem-bered all the times he could have chosen a different path, ended up different—and yet he didn't.

A person came flying at him. He was expecting Celia and could have easily batted her away. But what stunned him was that it was Naomi. She simply ran towards him, bloody hand coming off her hip. In a split second she had reached for the gun with both hands, pried it hard from his fingers. She yanked the gun away as if he were the child, and she swung back and struck him with it quickly, with force, across his eyes. It was hard enough to break his nose and split his forehead, blinding him with blood, and she followed with an immediate punch to his stomach. It felt like her hard fist had touched the inside of his spine, and he doubled over in pain. A dim part of him registered that this was the first time in his life anyone had ever struck *him*. Naomi knew body blows could take a man down. It was more painful than he could have imagined.

It was all happening too quickly. It wasn't supposed to be this way. Wesley fell to his knees, tried to get back up, only to receive a heart-stopping kick under the ribs that sent him sprawling in the soiled dirt. Another hard kick rocked his head back so far he felt his jaw break. With a decisive stomp Naomi landed on his right wrist, breaking it and causing him to scream in pain.

In agony Wesley rolled over, clutching his broken wrist, and he was looking through skeins of blood at the child he had once stolen. Naomi looked down at him. She lifted the gun. She was shaking, not from fear but from rage. The desire to hurt him came from a place so deep she felt it in her teeth. It was the healthiest thing she had ever felt.

"Naomi?" It was Celia.

From above came new noises. The front door was being battered in. The future entered the room.

Jerome dropped in the broken basement window, and in moments was gently taking the gun from Naomi, sliding on the safety, examining the wound at her hip. Winfield came rushing down the stairs to cuff Wesley, who was clutching his wrist in agony. Others were arriving, wrapping Celia in an insulated blanket.

Naomi was left alone, staring at her sister. The men pulled back.

Sarah was trying to make her mouth work, but it had been too long. Instead long sounds came out, as twisted as old cloth.

"You're going to be okay," Naomi told her sister, tears filling her mouth. All of her felt like one big cry. "I'll see to that."

I don't believe in revenge. But maybe I already had it."

This is what Naomi told Diane, who asked Naomi what she did believe in, only to be told prevention. Yet she knew that she had to go into the courtroom and speak the truth.

She walked through the polished courtroom doors, following the deputy. At tables were the district attorney—his forehead cried for mercy under the glare of lights—and a tired-looking public defender, willing to defend even this, his worst nightmare of a client, and Naomi understood that, too. We all deserve to know there is an outside. Even Wesley, sitting next to his public defender, a cast on his wrist.

Naomi strode to the front, and the deputy held the swinging gate to the witness box. The judge kept his eyes averted from the defendant, lest his contempt influence the jury.

Naomi met the jurors' eyes as she took the stand. She sat, tucked her one and only court skirt under her with her palms, straightened her back, and looked them right in the eye. Middle-aged school-teacher, she guessed. Mechanic. That one, with the nicotine hands? Retired. The angry-looking young man would be the hard one.

The oath. Naomi raised her hand. Her eyes were on the court clerk, but her warmth was for the jury. This parcel of humanity would decide what would happen to Wesley. The media would soon move on, but what was left behind had been so profound. The murdered street girls had all been identified. The unidentified migrant children in the graveyard had been exhumed, and a task force was at work locating their long-ago families. Teddy had been convicted for the sexual assault of Alyssa and was now serving time in prison. Alyssa was being adopted by her foster family—they had promised that Celia could visit as often as she wanted. Celia's mother . . . well, that was a longer story, and one that was not going to end soon.

And Celia? Naomi and Jerome were her new foster parents, and Celia lived in a room they had made for her in the attic. The walls were covered with her butterfly drawings. It had not been easy. Celia, left on her own so long, had almost feral characteristics. She hoarded food; she came and went as she pleased. The one way Naomi had discovered to get her to mind was the promise of a trip to the boxing gym. The fighters there called her Lil' Diablo.

But there was a lot of good all the same. Jerome had never smiled as much as when he saw Naomi and Celia together, walking home from the neighborhood library. Naomi had signed Celia up for the local school, where she was slowly making friends. Her favorite class was art, and at home she liked cooking with Diane.

Naomi had gone back to working missing child cases, and Jerome was building his own caseload—he was on the trail of a horrifying number of missing native women.

Even Rich had a home. He had gone to live at the horse track, where he had a little room above the stables. He was being trained by the Mexican man to work with the horses. He seemed happy, Celia had told Naomi.

Sometimes at night Naomi woke from sleep thinking, *We could have stopped it.* She hoped it was true, cordoned in the witness box, giving her small, careful answers to the jury. Yes, I was held captive by Wesley Thurman. Yes, I became an investigator to find missing children like myself.

And Celia.

Of all the events in her life this reverberated more than any. The green eyes, the willingness to fight. The courage. The joy in butterflies.

"Excuse me?" Just for a moment, she had faltered, and the district attorney repeated the question.

"I asked you, when you entered that home, who else did you find, held captive all these years?"

Naomi turned to the jury and let them see the pain in her eyes. "It was my sister."

* * *

Now Naomi was one of the people parking outside the state hospital, carrying a small plastic bag of quarters. As long as it takes, she had told the civil commitment board in a courthouse meeting. Her sister deserved the chance to heal. To discover her own reality, the path of a life that is chosen.

Perhaps for a magical reason, Sarah always waited at the same table. Naomi helped her feed quarters into the machine to get her a package of soft ginger cookies—Sarah loved sweets and couldn't get enough. After much dental surgery her mouth was healing, as was her ankle, broken and reset. Her mind would take longer. Holding an arm out, Naomi led Sarah outside. Sarah could now handle up to an hour of fresh air. She no longer cried out in pain from the touch of grass or the kiss of rain.

PTSD, the doctor had said. Dissociative disorder. Names like pillows trapped in trees. All Naomi saw was Sarah. Beloved, beautiful Sarah.

Sometimes Celia came with her. The psychiatrist said this would be healing to both of them. Naomi had her doubts. She didn't like the intimate looks they exchanged, as if sharing a secret past. Maybe it was jealousy. Naomi's own memories had stopped coming back. She was coming to terms with the fact they might never return, and that was okay. She didn't need to remember, Diane kept telling her.

Naomi led her sister to a plastic chair on a small patio outside. Sarah carefully lowered herself into the chair, turning around several times to make sure she got it right. Chairs were new to her. So was television. People. The sky. And noise from airplanes— the entire world seemed one earth-splitting scream—and tastes and smells. The smells of the world nauseated and delighted her in turn. She slept a lot. Sometimes the nurses found her in the hall closet, nestled under the coatrack.

Sarah smiled at Naomi. This was one reality she could trust. Big Sister had come back to her, just like she had promised. She had brought all their friends.

They sat in silence. They even sat the same way, legs open, shoulders back. Overhead fall clouds passed. The same trees that had budded were now shedding their leaves, getting ready for sleep. Rest here, Sarah. When you wake, you will be better.

Sarah's face was shifting, eyes awake and then vacant. "Whatever you want to tell me," Naomi had told her, "I will listen. There is nothing you can say that is wrong. I love you."

Sarah held her left arm out and opened her palm. She often did this when Naomi visited. Their eyes met, and Naomi smiled at her. Sarah turned to her own palm and her lips moved. She was telling her, or it, something, and this time Naomi could read a bit of her lips.

Sister, she was saying. Back.

* * *

The train rocked as it crossed the green hills, crowned with gold where the sun touched. To the north was a great river, and to the west even greater forests. This entire land was as old as time and as new as the dawn. Celia looked out the train window. In her mind her hands were pressed to the glass, like the child she once was but never had been.

"It's okay," Naomi had told her. "Grieve. Be all of you at once."

Naomi rode next to her, her body gently rocking with the train, her eyes closed. A peace had come over her. Celia could feel it.

Jerome knew it. Everyone who was around her felt it, even the nice detective who had come to Celia's welcome-home party.

A distant bell, a hooting. This was the world, too.

Naomi opened her eyes. The train slowed, and Celia and Naomi got off at a small, deserted station. They walked over a green hill to where a tall building stood alone, its windows recessed against the light.

Naomi stopped at the door, but Celia rushed forward.

She ran into the middle of a large room that rose to skylights of polished glass. The air was thick and warm with plants, with a smell that said forever.

All around her were the butterflies. Real butterflies! She spun, delighted. The soft, brilliant blue of a forester. A bright yellow of a cloudless sulfur, a white clearer than an eye, a green that trembled with life. Spicebush, tiger! The friendly eyes of a common wood nymph, a hotshot of a brassy red admiral. And who could forget the blue of a pipevine that runs east to west?

That was the sky.

From the doorway Naomi stood, smiling.

Celia raised her arms, and the laughter poured out. She clapped her hands in joy, and all around her the butterflies rose, fluttering against her skin, turning her silver with their dust. She lifted her head. For the first time in her life, she was unafraid.

She turned to Naomi, mouth open in delight.

Walking slowly, Naomi stepped into the room. The butterflies landed on her, too, caressing her skin. She felt them on her hair, her arms, her hands, which she raised to look at, covered with blurs of moving color.

The butterflies took flight, and they circled around her head: once, twice, three times. Like the rotation of the sun, they said thank you.

Reaching, Celia felt for Naomi's hand. She smiled at her.

"Now I know," she said.

"What?"

"Who I am."

ACKNOWLEDGMENTS

This book was raised by libraries and love. I wouldn't be a writer today if not for the public libraries of my difficult childhood, and the books that saved me with story. I will never forget the librarians of the downtown Portland, Oregon, library who expressed care for me when I, too, was a homeless kid. Thank you for showing me a path through the pain, and the beauty in the darkness.

Thank you to Luppi, Tony, Markel, Tamira, and to the other children I have been blessed to care for as a foster and adoptive mom. I am so lucky to be part of your journey. I love you beyond measure.

Thank you to my clients in my day job as a public defense investigator, including the trafficking victims, homeless, refugees, immigrants, veterans, and others who have filled my life. You have shared your pain with me, and I am honored to help you seek justice.

Thank you to my dear friends. This list is only partial: Stephanie, Sara, Alice, Andrea, Cheryl, Lidia, Karen, Julie, Mary, Laura,

Acknowledgments

Eric, Jen, Ellen, Samantha, Liz, Jane, Rhonda, Diana, Michele, Kelly, Monica, Kristi, Wendy, Nayomi, Dianah, Cece, DeAnn, Maggie, Sheila, Bette, Ronni, Mary, Pam, Rod, Monica, Sia, Jane, Angela, Leah, Jo, Scott, Anna, Kristina, Jenny, Joe, Gayle, Jackie, Bill, Susan, Marilyn, BJ, Skip, Shannon, Zoe, Cathy, Katie, Christopher, Cate, Bill, Kate, and all the fine folk at the Metropolitan Public Defender's Office. Thank you to Marty and Bill.

Thank you to my amazing team at HarperCollins: Gail, Doug, Tina, Rachel, Emily, Katie, Falon, John, Mary, and everyone else in Editorial, Production, Marketing, and Publicity. Thank you to Richard Pine, Eliza, Lyndsey, Nathaniel, and the wonderful folk at Inkwell. Thank you to Kirsty and Lettice for your valuable input, and Nicole Dewey for all the hard work.

And thank you, dear readers. Life is a story we tell ourselves and one another—we can make the story full of justice, kindness, and redemption. It's up to us.